SLOW BULLET II
THE LAST BULLET

SLOW BULLET II
THE LAST BULLET

JOHN L. LANSDALE

BOOKVOICE PUBLISHING

This book is a work of fiction. All incidents and all characters are fictionalized, with the exception that well-known historical and public figures are products of the author's imagination and are not to be construed as real. Where real-life historical figures appear, the situations and dialogues concerning those persons are fictional and are not intended to depict actual events within the fictional confines of the story. In all other respects, any resemblance to persons living or dead is entirely coincidental.

JOHN L. LANSDALE TITLES

-Broken Moon
-The Last Good Day
-Long Walk Home
-Beyond Imagination
-Kissing the Devil
-Slow Bullet
-The Complete Files of Detective Thomas Mecana
-Horse of a Different Color
-When the Night Bird Sings
-Twisted Justice
-The Box
-Zombie Gold
-Emergency Christmas
-Hell's Bounty [with Joe R. Lansdale]
-Shadows West [with Joe R. Lansdale]
-Tales from the Crypt (Comic Series)
-That Hellbound Train (Graphic Novel)
-Yours Truly, Jack the Ripper (Graphic Novel)

"Mickey Spillane fans will welcome this page-turner...Lansdale effectively delays revealing the novel's big secret until the end. Those who like their thrillers with a heavy dose of violent action will be satisfied." - Publishers Weekly review of Slow Bullet

"This is an entertaining, science fiction-historical-horror blend with resourceful protagonists and a solid cast of secondary characters."
- Booklist review of Zombie Gold

"Slow Bullet is a straight-ahead thriller...it's about action, and there's plenty of that. Check it out." - Bill Crider's Pop Culture Magazine

"...the author's innate ability to spin a complex tale painted with vivid characters and intense suspense provides readers with a well-paced book that they may find difficult to set down...a worthwhile suspenseful ride." - Amazing Stories review of Horse of a Different Color

"Has something for everyone... It's exciting, entertaining and educational. A fun ride."
- TV personality Joan Hallmark, review of Zombie Gold

"...something unique and comfortable and difficult to put down. Highly recommended." - Cemetery Dance review of Hell's Bounty

"True to Lansdale tradition, John L. Lansdale has compiled a piece of work that should appeal to a wide range of readers."
- Amazing Stories review of Zombie Gold

"Long Walk Home really touched and gripped me. A great bittersweet story of light and shadow about growing up in a time gone by. I loved it." - author Joe R. Lansdale

For
Ricky & Jackie

For everything gained something is lost.
Author

1

On my get out of town flight from Washington, D.C. to Paris, France, my seat-mate, a bald-headed middle-aged man wearing glasses, introduced himself as Richard, a big movie fan from Kansas, and asked me if I wanted to watch The Godfather with him. I nodded yes and we watched Marlon Brando, with his mouth full of cotton, give his memorable performance. There were parts I could identify with. I had evened the score some for the murder of my best friend, his wife, son and my comrades on the Vietnam Wall before I headed for Paris.

A cute little blonde flight attendant with Cindy on her name tag stopped at my seat with a big airline smile.

"Would you like a drink, Mr. McKay," she said.

She knew my name. She must have been looking at the manifest. Why? It made me wonder if the bad guys were after me before I got back on the ground.

"A Coke," I said.

She scooped some ice in a glass and pointed to a Jack Daniels bottle. I shook my head no. My need for whiskey was not as strong as it used to be but I knew I could never have another drink for the rest of my life. She poured the Coke into the glass and handed it to me and sat the empty can on her cart.

"How did you know my name?" I asked.

"The first class passenger manifest lists a Clark McKay. Your friend Martinez stopped me when I was getting on the plane," she said. "He told me you were a VIP and to take good care of you."

Martinez wasn't a friend. He was a crooked CIA agent sending me a message.

"Is he on the plane?"

"No. How about you, sir," she said, looking at Richard. "You want a drink?"

"Maybe later," Richard said.

She gave us another smile and pushed her cart on down the aisle. After drinking my Coke and watching Godfather with Richard, I turned to the starboard window and gazed out at the rain clouds gathering around the airplane. I pulled the shade down and dozed off to sleep not long after that, Vietnam nightmares invading my sleep.

A squadron of Huey helicopters roared across the sky like locusts, firing rockets into enemy positions. Vietcong mortars whistled back at us. It was a nightmare I repeatedly had for years, from a successful bloody battle I led in the Mekong Valley to take back a fire base where the NVA had overrun and killed everyone. Mostly young soldiers in their twenties. I could still see them in my dreams.

Suddenly, I woke up in a cold sweat, turbulence bouncing the aircraft around like a toy. The plane dropped several feet, scaring the hell out of everyone on board before the pilot could stabilize it. I raised the shade and looked out the window. We were flying through black mushy clouds, rain dancing on the wings like a high-speed car wash.

The pilot's voice came on the intercom assuring us everything was fine, to buckle our seatbelts, and that we would be landing in seventeen minutes.

Cindy made her way down the aisle holding on to the seats, checking everyone to see if they had their seatbelts on.

"You alright, Mr. McKay?" she said.

"I'm fine."

"You were twisting in your seat before the turbulence woke you up."

"Bad dream," I said. "I got my belt on."

"Was it a movie," Richard asked.

"No a war," I said.

"A war movie?"

"No, a real one."

"Can I get you anything?" Cindy asked, looking at us both.

"No thank you," I said. Richard shook his head no and she turned back toward the cockpit and walked away.

Richard was staring at me. "She said you were a VIP. You an actor?"

"No," I said.

"Oh, so you're not a VIP."

I grinned and shook my head no. "Only to myself."

He nodded back and started punching his remote at the dead TV in front of him.

When we touched down I said goodbye to Cindy and Richard, picked up my baggage and called my wife's sister Billie. She said she was on her way to the airport with my newly-inherited Jack Russell terrier Scooter I got from my murdered best friend Robert.

I had a short visit with Billie about two months ago when I was in Switzerland; she had a picture I sent her years ago and it turned out to be what I needed to find who killed Robert Spicier and his wife Elle. She invited me back and this was the best time to go—after my encounters with the Parkers, my double-crossing friend Sam, and corrupt CIA agents.

As I stepped out on the airport sidewalk to wait for Billie, it was like turning back the pages of time.

I remembered being assigned to the embassy in Paris as a captain attaché way back when and where I met my beautiful wife Mary. Her dad was a US diplomat at the embassy. Mary was an English teacher at an exclusive French school like her mother. The only difference was her mother was French. I was immediately struck by Mary's beauty and intellect. I found out later she had been a college beauty queen during her time in the USA.

We fell madly in love and got married six months after I arrived in Paris. After my son Cooper was born we transferred back to the States. Mary taught him French at an early age for her mother. He was attending the Air Force Academy with the intent to become a jet fighter pilot, following in his daddy's military footsteps, only in the air instead of on the ground.

The pain of their unexpected deaths in a car wreck drove me to booze. I became a drunk for years until I woke up in a stupor one morning in a jail cell with another drunk and saw a vision of Mary the way she looked the day she drove away to never return. It's a vision that haunts me everyday. I haven't had a drink since.

A black Mercedes pulled up and stopped a few feet from me. Two men got out dressed in black suits. Dead ringers for CIA agents but not the ones I knew. They gave me a quick glance and walked inside the airport. I kept an eye out for their return, or anyone giving me too much visual attention, as I continued to wait for Billie.

A white BMW SUV appeared slowing down and stopped where I was standing. Scooter was looking out the car window. I opened the door and he jumped in my arms. We had become quick buddies. I think we both sensed the need for each other. I put my baggage in the back seat and held Scooter on the way to Billie's place with him licking my face to show how much he missed me. The feeling was mutual.

We stopped at a sidewalk café for dinner. I sat Scooter on a chair and ordered him a French hamburger that he didn't like very much but was hungry enough to eat it in slow bites. Billie and I ate a salad and reminisced about Mary and Cooper for the first time since they were killed five years ago when my world fell apart. Billie thought it was my fault at the time because Mary went to the airport to pick up Cooper instead of me. She apologized and hugged my neck. I didn't know what to say. She paid the bill and we seemed to run out of conversation as she drove home.

I was sure she meant her apology. She was three years younger than Mary, with the same beauty. She had several boyfriends over the years but never found one she wanted to spend her life with. During that time she became an international artist, earning big money for her paintings. Over the years she came to visit us many times in the States and spent a lot of time with Cooper when he was a teenager, teaching him how to paint.

Two of his paintings are still hanging on the wall in our house that I haven't been to in some time. My old lawyer friend's son is taking care of it for me. He's a policeman, ten years older than Cooper. Should have sold the house but couldn't bring myself to do it.

Cooper would have graduated second in his class at West Point three months after he came home if he hadn't died. He said he had a girlfriend, didn't tell me the name, and I didn't try to find her when she didn't show up for the funeral.

Billie had a nice room ready for me when we got to her house. After a shower I got in bed and, with Scooter curled up beside me, slept without any nightmares and felt better the next morning.

I saw a note on the kitchen table. Billie said she had to go to an art show and would be back in three or four hours. There was a place down the street to eat. I walked in the bathroom and looked at the man in the mirror. I needed a shave and a gun. I could let my hair and beard grow long as a disguise, but my pride rejected that thought. I still had the physical ability to defend myself, or at least I thought so, which was good for a man in his late sixties. I dismissed the concern and cleaned up and shaved.

I put Scooter under my arm walked outside on the cobbled streets and hailed a taxi. Dark clouds were moving in. I noticed the worn smoothness of the cobbled streets that were made from thousands of people walking them for centuries. A quick lesson in French history with a glance. I got in the taxi with Scooter in my arms and told the driver "McDonald's."

The taxi driver looked back at me over the seat and repeated what I said. "McDonalds restaurant, monsieur?"

I nodded yes and he pulled out into the street, dodging another taxi. He readjusted his bare black seat to an angle he liked, twitched his pencil-thin black mustache and stroked his pointed chin. He looked like he had just stepped out of a Pepé Le Pew cartoon.

After we ate and got back to Billie's, a furious crack of thunder jarred the windows. Lightning flashed across the sky and a downpour followed. Seemed like a good time for me and Scooter to take a nap.

My cell phone rang. It was Nina from the International Bank of Switzerland.

"Mr. McKay," she said. "I checked like you asked. Your power of attorney has been cleared and the bank can release Mr. Spicier's account to you. You can leave the money here or transfer it to an account of your choice."

"Thank you," I said and hung up. I contemplated what to do with the money from my dead friend's account in Switzerland. His daughter Pepper didn't want it because it was dirty money and I didn't either because it was once Elton Parker's—a global scoundrel. It occurred to me my friend Sandy, who always helped me when I needed it, didn't have a reason to not like it. Now it was my turn to return the favor. I called her.

"Hi, Clark," Sandy said. "I didn't expect to hear from you so soon."

"I didn't expect to call so soon. Anyone bothered you?"

"No. I think you convinced them to leave me and Mary Ann

alone."

Hearing her speak about her daughter Mary always gave me a warm feeling because of her pretty little girl and my Mary.

"You alright?" Sandy asked.

"Yeah, I want to send Mary Ann a birthday present."

"Her birthday is four months away."

"Alright, then this is a pre-birthday gift."

"If that's what you want to do."

"I do. You have a bank account?"

"Yes, but if you're sending money you can wire it directly to me."

"I'd like to send it to your bank account," I said. "Safer that way if you already have one."

"Makes sense," she said. "You got a pen?"

"Yep, go," I said and wrote down her account information.

"My daughter and I will be waiting for you when you get back," she said.

"You'll be the first ones I come see. Check your bank account tomorrow. It should be there by then."

"I'll call you," she said. "Talk to you tomorrow."

I called Nina back at the Switzerland bank and transferred five million dollars with my power of attorney from Robert's bank account in Switzerland to Sandy Wiggins' account at the First National Bank in Long Shore, New York.

Parker's orphan blood money had finally found a good home.

I laid down on the couch; Scooter on the white shaggy rug. The lightning and thunder kept doing their thing and the rain was coming down in buckets. I dozed off to sleep.

Later, I woke up having trouble breathing. I noticed Scooter was throwing up on the rug while I was gasping for breath. I tried to get up but fell back down on the couch. I couldn't see. It was like a black curtain had been pulled down over my eyes and the sound of the rain seemed far away. The room was spinning. I kept going in and out of consciousness. Someone was shaking my arm, saying something I couldn't understand.

Through the swirling blackness it came to me.

Trilene.

"Junior, you son of a bitch."

There was nothing I could do. He used the same weapon on me he had used on Robert.

There was no defense for it.

My life was over.

2

Two days passed before I woke up. The first thing I saw was Billie smiling at me.

"Welcome back," she said.

"Where am I?" I asked.

"In the hospital. Thank god I got you here in time."

"My dog?"

"He had trouble breathing but he's okay now. The police are checking my place for any other traces of Trilene. Me and Scooter are staying with a friend. I packed your stuff and got some of mine. I don't know how long we will have to stay at my friend's house."

"How do you know about Trilene?" I asked.

"I heard you say it and cuss somebody named Junior so I googled it. Who's Junior?"

"He's the son of Elton Parker, the kingpin of corruption and mob bosses in Washington, D.C. He won't give up trying to kill me until I kill him."

"Pepper called while you were out," Billie said. "I answered it. She said Trilene killed her mom and dad and that was what was happening here. She called about every two hours to check on you until I told her you were going to make it. This is unbelievable. If I hadn't got back when I did you would be dead. You were lucky on top of that. The police lab told me the rain blowing moisture in the air vents diluted the poison and slowed the effect down."

"What can I say, I owe you big time. As soon as I get on my feet I'll head back to the States to eliminate Junior and his friends."

"You mean kill them?"

"Yeah, that's what I mean. Don't have a choice. They would kill you in the blink of an eye out of spite if I stayed here."

My phone started ringing but I couldn't reach it.

"I got it," Billie said and picked up the phone. "You want to talk to Sandy? She's called a hundred times in the last two days. I didn't answer it. Don't know her. Wasn't sure if I should or not."

I held my hand out and she handed me the phone.

"Hello," I said.

"Clark, what the hell is going on?" Sandy said through the phone. "I thought you were dead."

"I almost was."

"What happened? I been trying to call you for days."

"I had some problems but I'm okay now," I said. "You get the money?"

"Where the hell did you get all that money and why did you send it to me?"

"I'm going to be coming back soon. We'll talk about it then, just don't tell anyone you have it in the meantime."

"I need to know what's going on now, not later," she said.

"Trust me, it's okay. I'll tell you all about it when I get there. Go buy you and Mary Ann something nice. It's yours to keep."

"I'll wait until you get here," she said. "You scared the hell out of me."

"I'll try to get a flight out tomorrow. Quit worrying."

"Call me as soon as you know when you will be here," she said and hung up.

"What's that all about?" Billie asked.

"I sent her a lot of money she deserved. It's complicated. Get me out of here and we can talk later."

"I think they want to keep you a while longer," she said. "You had a seizure last night, jerking your arms and legs. They have to run more tests."

"Must have been something in the Trilene. Only thing I remember is my 'Nam nightmares and the train chase when the Sanfinis tried to kill me. I got to get out of here. Where's my clothes?"

"You should stay here until they know what's happening to you," Billie said.

"I hate to get up from here and walk out with my ass showing from the back of this gown but that's what I'm going to do if I can't find my clothes."

Billie walked over to a cabinet, reached in and picked up my clothes and tossed them to me. "Your shoes are under the bed, get dressed," she said.

"I have to go," I said, putting on my clothes.

"I'll get the car," Billie said. "Call Pepper before we leave, she'll be calling the hospital. We'll have to go to my friends. I'm having a new air and heating system put in the bungalow to clean it. You shouldn't do this but I know how hard-headed you are. Once you set your mind on something there's no turning back."

"That's true," I said.

"Go out an exit so they won't know you're gone. Watch for me out front," Billie said. "Call Pepper and let her know what you're doing," she said again and hurried out of the room.

I dialed Pepper and she answered. "Clark, are you okay?"

"Thanks to Billie I think I'm going to be."

"That's great. Do you need anything?" she said.

"No, I'm going to make an escape from the hospital and book a flight home. I'm afraid if I stay here they will murder me and Billie."

"Wouldn't put it past them. Let me know when you get here and I'll pick you up."

"I'm going to Long Shore first to get Sandy and her kid out of there. They'll be coming after her. And you, too. Stay with Matt."

"He's not here anymore. We split up."

"Sorry to hear that," I said.

"I'm alright. It just didn't work out."

"Watch your back, then. I'll see you in the next day or two."

"Don't worry, I can take care of myself."

"I'll amen that."

We said our goodbyes and hung up.

After getting dressed, I opened my room door and looked out into the hall and saw an exit sign. I rushed across the hall to the door, lifted the safety rod, opened the door and ran around to the front. Billie's SUV was waiting in the hospital entrance driveway. I opened the door and got in.

"Who's this friend you were talking about?" I asked. She pulled out of the driveway on a street.

"We've known each other a long time. He's a painter, too. Went to art school together."

"He's French?"

"Yes. His name's Clarence," Billie said. "Kind of a boyfriend, too, if you know what I mean."

"Yeah, I know what you mean. You're having sex but it leaves you the option to be alone when you want to."

"That's crude," Billie said. "But it's true. We love each other. Met many years ago in art school. Never got around to thinking about getting married. Now at this point in our life it's better to keep things the way they are."

"I didn't know how to sugarcoat it," I said and grinned.

"It's okay," Billie said.

"I wouldn't be alive if it wasn't for you. Thank you. I seem to bring trouble wherever I go."

"Why don't you turn this over to the police?"

"Tried that. It didn't work. Parker's got too much power."

"I wish there was some other way," she said. "But I know you would go there if there was."

"Thanks for the confidence."

"We're almost to Clarence's place. What about Scooter? Want me to keep him?"

"I'll pass him off as a therapy seizure dog. Get him a seat. Saw seizures on my medical chart, grabbed it before I took off. Don't want him in the cargo hold."

"You don't let anything stop you from what you think you should do," Billie said. "Have you had anymore seizures?"

"No—Oh hell, spoke too soon. Pull over and stop, I'm going to throw up."

Billie whipped the car off the road and stopped. I opened the door, leaned out and threw up a mass of green slime.

"You should have stayed in the hospital," Billie said. "You're not over this."

"Better now," I said. "Go on."

"Did you hear me?"

"Doesn't matter. I have to do what I have to do."

"Those may be your famous last words. You realize you're not a spring chicken any more?"

"Yep, but I'm going to keep crowing until I can't."

Billie smiled and turned into a driveway. "We're here," she said. "Good luck."

"I'm going to need it," I said. "You're a doll. Thanks. You always remind me of Mary. Your family had it all."

"That's a compliment I will never forget," Billie said and opened her door. "Your dog is waiting for you."

"We've been through a lot together."

"What if they won't let you book Scooter?"

"They will. I got the proof in my pocket."

"You going to D.C.?" Billie asked.

"No. Long Shore, New York to see Sandy first. I'll have her pick me up. I have to make sure she and her daughter are okay before I go back to D.C. My fault she's had trouble with the Parkers. May have to keep them under my wing for a while."

"Or under the covers," Billie said and grinned.

"Don't think so. Just a friend. Better call for a flight. You stay with your friend for a while so they will know I'm gone."

"If you survive all this come back," Billie said.

"I will." I leaned over and pecked Billie on the cheek. She smiled.

The house was big. Her friend had money. The front door opened and a small thin man walked out of the house. He had a full head of black hair with some gray on his temples, age wrinkles on his face and a pencil-thin mustache, a Frenchman's favorite. He had a red and gray ascot wrapped around his neck, wearing a red sweater and sharp, creased gray pants. He was smiling when he opened the driver's door for Billie. She got out and they hugged and gave each other a quick kiss. I got out and walked around to the other side of the car. He walked up to me. I could have raised my arms straight out and he could have walked under them with my six-two height. We had the hair and age in common, minus the mustache. He stuck out his hand and we shook hands.

"Billie said someone poisoned you, Mr. McKay."

"They did," I said. "Thank you for your help."

"My pleasure. You kin to Billie you kin to me. Your dog and bag is in the room I prepared for you. I understand you're flying back to the States in the morning?"

"Yes I am. Take care of Billie for me."

"Oh I will. We have been doing that for each other for along time. Come on in and I'll show you to your room." He spoke perfect English without a hint of a French accent.

I nodded and we went in the house.

3

Billie dropped me and Scooter off at the airport the next morning around ten to give us time to check in for our departure an hour later. They let me book Scooter as a therapy dog after I showed the hospital chart. But we could only book in the passenger section. No first class. The flight was supposed to arrive in Long Shore, New York a little before one in the afternoon after a seven hour, forty-eight minute flight. Too long to babysit Scooter on an airplane but too late to change it now. They said I had to have a diaper on Scooter when I got on the plane. I took off my shirt, tied it on his bottom and put my jacket back on my bare chest and zipped it up. We both would be stinking by the time we got to Long Shore. He sat down on the seat next to me. I fastened his seat belt that wouldn't do any good and he stuck his head under my arm and looked at a fat man

29

sitting across the aisle from us and growled. The fat man was wearing a Hawaiian shirt as big as a tent and was flashing his brown beady eyes at us under his straw hat. Him and Scooter were having a stare-down. The fat man raised his arm up, made a fist and shook it at the dog.

"He won't bite you," I said.

"He better not," he said. "I'll knock his head off."

"Mister, you hit my dog and the undertaker will wipe your ass."

An elderly lady with white hair sitting next to him on a window seat gasped and turned to the window.

"That's a terrible thing to say. I could have you arrested," he said and dropped his arm down beside his body. "You shouldn't have brought a dog on board."

"Quit staring at him and he will quit staring at you," I said.

The fat man turned his head away. Scooter took the cue. He laid down, snuggled up to my leg and went to sleep for over two hours before waking up and staring at the fat man again. But the fat man didn't know, he was snoring. Scooter gave it up and went back to sleep.

Later on they brought us some bad airline steak dinners. They woke the fat man up to my dismay to feed him. He chomped on the food like a wild animal and it was gone in minutes. His seat partner nibbled at her food, glancing at Scooter a few times, and pushed the seat back from the food and turned on her side to the window. The fat man finished off a beer and went back to sleep without a word.

Me and scooter choked down a few bites. When he turned away from it I knew it was as bad as I thought it was. I poured Scooter water in a paper cup and held it for him to drink. He drank some and went back to sleep.

We didn't have anymore trouble.

We landed on schedule in Long Shore, New York. I got off the plane carrying Scooter under my arm. I pulled the shirt off his butt and dropped the soiled makeshift diaper in the trash. Wouldn't ever do that again. I called Pepper and told her I was in

Long Shore and would call her as soon as I got to Goodnight's in D.C.

"I'll be waiting," she said.

Sandy and Mary Ann were waiting for us at the end of the walkway from the plane.

Scooter started wagging his tail. He remembered Sandy and Mary Ann. They walked up to us.

"Scooter," Mary Ann said and Scooter started twisting in my arms. I sat him down, holding on to the leash, and he started licking Mary Ann.

"Can I lead him, Mr. McKay?" Mary Ann said.

"Sure," I said and handed her the leash.

Sandy looked at my hand as I was handing the leash to Mary Ann and saw my missing little finger on my right hand.

"I forgot they cut your finger off," she said.

"Yeah the Sanfini mob bunch for Parker. They would have been smarter to cut my trigger finger off. The one that did it is dead."

"What happened to him?" she said.

"I killed him."

She looked stunned stared at me for a moment. "We better get out of here," she said.

Sandy moved in front of me wearing a designer white pants suit, her long blonde curls hanging on her shoulders, bright red fingernails and red high-heels. I stepped back from her to avoid putting a smell on her.

"We stink," I said, motioning to Scooter.

"I don't care," she said. She rubbed up against me, wrapped her arms around my neck and planted a big kiss on me.

"Am I glad to see you." She looked down at Mary Ann and Scooter. "I didn't think Scooter would remember us."

"I did," I said and grinned.

"You're a true optimist," Sandy said.

"Mary Ann, hold on to Scooter and I'll get my bags," I said. We walked down the corridor to the elevator and took a ride down to the luggage floor.

An hour later, we pulled into Sandy's driveway in her red Honda. The same car she had when we met that I had to buy tires for after Elton Parker's son—Brandon Twotree—shot out all four tires. Had to beat the hell out of him, leaving him on the side of the road. Didn't know if he was still around after I killed his daddy, setting it up to look like a suicide. For good reason. The cops haven't figured it out yet. Not enough evidence to arrest me. Pepper is the only one that knows what really happened, although I think Goodnight has put the pieces together. Don't think he wanted to talk about it. I didn't either.

Sandy's rented house looked about the same from what I could see in the dark.

Mary Ann and Scooter were loving on each other when we went in. I may have found Scooter a better home after all, I thought and sat my bag down, Sandy standing beside me.

"Can I take the leash off Scooter now, Mr. McKay?" Mary Ann asked.

"Just make sure the doors and windows are closed."

I unsnapped the leash and Scooter started running through the house.

"Mary Ann needs a better name for you than Mr. McKay," Sandy said.

"How about Clark," I said.

"Not right for a child," Sandy said.

"You come up with something," I said. "I need to unwind a little from the flight. Direct me to a shower and I'll get me and Scooter cleaned up and explain the money."

"I hope so, that's been driving me nuts thinking about all that money."

"It's your's and Mary Ann's, no strings attached."

"I want to hear more. Fill in the blanks for me. You don't just give someone that kind of money without there being a story behind it."

"Later," I said. "Where's the shower?"

"Come with me," she said, walking away. I picked up my bag and followed.

"You want me to scrub your back?" she said and smiled.

"I'll manage," I said.

"Me and Mary Ann will give Scooter a quick bath," she said. "I put two towels on the rack for you. Shampoo and soap on the side of the tub."

After she left the bathroom, I undressed and turned on the water, adjusting the temperature. Suddenly, a bloodcurdling scream jumped through the walls at me. I turned off the water, wrapped a towel around me and hurried out of the bathroom.

Sandy was on the floor, naked from the waist up, fighting off a man on the floor. His back was to me. Mary Ann was screaming, hitting him in the back with her fists and pulling on his long, stringy blonde hair; Scooter biting his arm. He swung his arm backwards and knocked Mary Ann across the floor. He jerked Sandy's suit pants down, trying to pull them off. She was trying to reach one of her red high-heel shoes for a weapon.

I ran up behind him and put a chokehold on him, locking his arms over his head and jerked him off his feet, dangling in my arms like a puppet. A cellphone fell out of his shirt pocket. A strong whiskey smell reminded me of my old friend Jack Daniels. Sandy back-peddled away from him on the floor holding her torn blouse with one hand and holding Mary Ann with the other hand, watching us. I dropped the man to the floor and my towel fell off. I was naked as a jaybird. He sat up, looked at my naked body and blinked several times. He had a Colt stuffed in his belt. I bent down and snatched it out of his belt before he could get it.

"What are you doing with my wife," he said.

"Your wife?" I looked at Sandy, picked up the towel and wrapped it around me, still holding on to the Colt. "This your husband, Sandy?"

"Used to be," Sandy said.

"You still my wife, bitch. We never got a divorce. I can legally have you when I want to."

"You ain't playing with a full deck are you?" I said.

"You're that McKay guy, ain't you? Brandon told me all about you. You murdered his daddy. Kiss my ass, old man. You ain't telling me nothing."

I jerked his belt loose and pulled it off him. "Put your hands behind your back," I said and pointed the Colt at him.

"You wouldn't shoot me," he said.

"All your ex-wife has to do is say pull the trigger and you're dead."

He glanced at Sandy, then the Colt. I cocked the hammer. He leaned forward like he was going to fall and pushed a leg out to brace himself. He put his hands behind his back. I tied his hands, ripped the sleeve off his shirt off and stuffed it in his mouth. He started kicking at me, spinning around on his butt. Scooter nipped at his legs.

"Here," I said and handed Sandy the Colt. "Stay out of his reach. If he moves, shoot him. I'll get dressed."

He did a quick look at Sandy. "You better let me go, bitch, or I'll kill you."

"One more word out of you and I'll kill you." She backed away and shook the gun at him. "I know you stole this. You wouldn't pay for it."

I looked back over my shoulder, holding the towel to keep it from slipping off, and walked into the bathroom. I took a quick rinse, dried off, got dressed and rushed back to Sandy, taking the gun back.

"I'll call Sonny," I said, "and see what he can do with him. Then we'll get out of here."

"He know you're back?" Sandy said.

"No." I dialed Sonny.

He picked up after a few rings. "Lieutenant Goodnight," he said.

"Hey, it's me," I said.

"Hey, McKay, how you doing in Paris?" Sonny said.

"I'm back home. They tried to kill me with Trilene."

"You should have stayed there regardless. You had a better chance," he said.

"Don't think so, they would have murdered my sister-in-law."

"What you going to do now?" he said.

"Sandy's ex, Neil Wiggins, showed up drunk, tried to rape her. I made a citizen's arrest. Going to bring him to you."

"I don't have jurisdiction to arrest him. Take him to the local police. Have her file a complaint for his arrest."

"They would turn him loose," I said. "Brandon is his drinking buddy."

"You have to turn him loose. He can have you arrested for kidnapping. We'll find something to get him on later. Speaking of Brandon, he did you a favor while you were gone. A regular dumbass. He burned Elton Parker's mansion down to the ground, taking evidence of Parker's death with it before they had enough evidence to indict you."

"No shit?" I said.

"Yeah, the county sheriff tried to arrest him for arson. Brandon said it was his, he could do what he wanted. The old man did will it to him and his Indian mother. They found a will in his D.C. office and dropped the charges, just gave him a small fine for reckless burning. The mansion was the only thing his daddy gave him. Junior got all the rest. Just get the hell out of there and bring Sandy and the girl, we'll figure out what to do next."

"How's your leg?" I said.

"A lot better. Other than the two bullet scars I'll have the rest of my life."

"Big deal, I got a dozen."

"Doesn't surprise me," he said. "I think I'll be able to go back to work next week. Julie and the kids are getting tired of me staying home so much."

"I'll turn Wiggins loose when I get out of town. See you tomorrow. I'll call when I get there."

"Leave now," Sonny said.

"We will," I said.

Sandy came back from her bedroom wearing a shirt, jeans and sneakers.

"We can't take him to Goodnight," I said. "I'm going to leave him here. By the time he gets loose we'll be long gone." I jerked the cord out of a lamp, wrapped it around his ankles and tied his legs together. "That ought to slow you down."

"I don't want to leave my things here," Sandy said.

"You can buy more. We have to leave. Maybe you can get a moving company to get the rest later."

"Okay," she said. "I'll grab us some clothes and we'll go."

She went to the bedroom threw some clothes for her and Mary Ann in a suitcase and returned to the front room.

"I'm ready," she said and opened the front door.

Wiggins was lying on the floor. You could see the hate in his eyes.

I carried their bags to the car, Mary Ann carrying Scooter to the back door on the passenger side. Sandy closed the door. Sandy opened the front passenger door and got in. I walked around the car to the driver door and got in under the wheel, starting the Honda, and we headed for D.C.

I whipped the car around a truck and put the pedal to the metal. At an intersection a sign read Washington, D.C. - 367 miles with an arrow pointing to the left. I made a left turn on the highway.

"You think they will ever leave you alone?" Sandy asked.

"No, don't think so. They know I won't leave them alone, either. I'll have to take them all down on my own before it's over."

"That sounds gruesome," Sandy said.

"It is. I've been thinking about you and Mary Ann. You would be better off to get away from me. Take your money and disappear somewhere safe. Don't even tell me."

"Only way I would do that was if you came with us," she said.

"That's a good offer but with me that's not a good solution. Get some sleep, we got a long drive."

"I think I'm wound up too tight," Sandy said "I'll help you stay awake until we get there."

"Okay, tell me your life's story."

"Too boring."

"Tell me anyway," I said.

"Goodnight told me a lot about you," she said.

"Big mouth," I said.

"What you want to know about me," she said.

"Does Wiggins know about the money?"

"I don't think so. He would already be trying to take it away from me."

4

We stopped to get a hamburger and hit the road again. Around five the next morning we were on the outskirts of D.C. I woke up Goodnight with a phone call and told him we were on our way to his house. Didn't look like we had a tail.

"I'll be waiting for you," he said.

Mary Ann and Scooter zonked out in the back seat and Sandy was curled up in the front seat, also asleep. I thought about what she told me during the drive.

Her ex was a real loser, stayed drunk. Reminded me of myself. They never got a divorce. He still had a legal right to half her money. She said she married Neil Wiggins ten years ago. Her dad was a soldier killed in Iraq in1993. Her mom was a chain smoker who died of lung cancer shortly after using every penny from selling her house and the Army insurance. Nothing had been left for Sandy and her kid.

Sandy had said Neil showed up in Long Shore to see his sister June that worked with her at Ma's Pies Café after he got out of the Marines the same year her mother died. She said she never knew where the rest of his family was. He got a job as the manager of a hardware store.

They started dating and got married. Everything seemed good for three years except he was drinking too much. Mary Ann was born and she thought that would settle him down but it didn't. He started staying out late every night getting drunk at The Idle Hour Bar with Brandon. He had too many mornings he woke up too drunk to go to work and got fired. He forced her to give him her check every week. She would have to beg for money to take care of Mary Ann and herself.

She moved out and rented the house she was living in now. Neil came to the house and begged her for another chance and she let him move in. He got a job at the Idle Hour as a bartender. The worst place he could work. He started getting drunk again with Brandon Parker. Brought one of the prostitutes from the bar home one night wanting to have sex with her and Sandy at the same time. She told Mary Ann to go to her room and not come out. She hit him with a lamp and he beat her unconscious with his fist. When she woke up, they were gone with what little jewelry she had, including her wedding ring and money from her purse. She didn't want Mary Ann to know what happened with her daddy so she never called the cops, told Mary Ann she fell down, knowing Mary Ann had heard enough of the arguments from her room to know he did it. She called in sick to Ma's Pies to let the swelling in her face go down.

After three days she went back to work. Neil's sister June had quit and no one knew where she was. After work her first day back, Sandy picked up Mary Ann at school and went home, confused about what to do. She finally decided to call Curly at the Idle Hour to see if Neil or his sister was there. Curly said he hadn't seen June for two or three weeks but Neil stopped by driving June's car about three days ago. Said he didn't see June in the car when he looked out a window but Neil had a beer at the bar, said he quit and was going back to the Marines and left.

That's the last anyone in Long Shore saw him or his sister. Until he showed up at Sandy's last night. I knew we would see him again.

When I pulled in the driveway a light was on in the house. I shook Sandy's arm and she woke up.

"We're here," I said and she sat up.

"No one following us," she said, rubbing her eyes looking around.

"Don't think so," I said.

The porch light came on and Sonny opened the door dressed in jeans and a t-shirt, his black hair combed in the middle as usual and his trimmed mustache, with an automatic in his hand. He waved it for us to come in and cut the porch light off, holding the door open. I got out, closed the driver door and opened the back door. Scooter jumped out. I picked up a sleeping Mary Ann and we went in the house. Sonny closed the front door, latched it, and limped to a floral-covered chair. He sat down still holding the automatic in his hand.

"Have a seat," he said and laid the automatic on a table next to the chair. Mary Ann woke up when I sat her down on the couch and me and Sandy sat down with her.

"Where's the boys, Mr. Goodnight," Mary Ann said.

"They're still asleep," Goodnight said. "Go wake them, second door on the right." He waved his hand to the right to show her and she and Scooter took off down the hall.

"Julie's getting dressed," Goodnight said.

"I shouldn't have come. I'm sorry," I said. "I'm disrupting your family."

"Hey, I know what you been through. I'm in your corner."

"I appreciate that, but it's not your fight, Sonny. Help me find a place for Sandy and Mary Ann. I'll disappear."

"Why can't you arrest them," Sandy said, looking at Goodnight.

"It gets complicated, Sandy," Sonny said. "Clark may have

charges coming up against him. Makes it more difficult. I had FBI agents stop by the office the other day, found your fingerprints on the CIA file you sent them. They were pretty shook up about the contents, said it should be put to rest, that most of the people involved were already dead. They tracked you to France. Asked me where they could find you. I really didn't know where and that's what I told them and they left. They'll know you're back."

"I think they already found me. Miracle I'm still here."

Scooter came running out of the boys' bedroom and jumped up in my lap, staring at me.

"That dog really took to you," Sonny said.

"Yeah, I—oh shit—the room's spinning."

It felt like I was going down. I tried to stand up but my knees buckled and I fell to the floor, pain running through my head, and passed out.

Next thing I knew, I was in a hospital bed hours later looking at the ceiling, hooked up to monitors. Sandy and Sonny were sitting next to the bed, Sandy holding my hand. She saw I was awake.

"You passed out, Clark. Was jerking your legs and arms, rolling on the floor. They think you had an epileptic seizure."

A middle-aged man walked in the room wearing a white coat with a stethoscope around his neck, Dr. West on his name tag, his thin gray hair neatly combed with a short gray goatee. He walked up to the bed and looked down at me.

"How you doing?" he said, taking the stethoscope from around his neck, putting the plugs in his ears and placing it on my heart.

"Better," I said.

He nodded, listened to my heartbeat for a few seconds, then dropped the stethoscope back around his neck.

"Your heart's strong," he said. "I think you're over the seizure."

"What happened to me?" I said.

"You don't know you have epilepsy?" he said.

"No."

"That's what the tests show. You've been in an accident, hit your head?"

"No, but someone tried to kill me with Trilene in France a few days ago by putting it in the air vents. It's the same drug that killed my friend Robert Spicier and his wife Ellie. Thank goodness my sister-in-law should up in time to save me. They said I had a seizure at the hospital. I don't remember that one, either. This morning, though, I damn sure remember."

"That explains the seizures," the doctor said, "because the drug is designed to put you in a comfortable unconsciousness state for medical reasons, or kill you if you're given too much. Trilene is the short name for it. The complete medical name is Trichloroethylene. An overdose would damage your nervous system, which sounds like what happened from what you said. The effect wears off quickly and the odor disappears. You need a counter-drug that will stop the seizures."

"I saw it kill my best friend and his wife," I said.

"That's horrible. They ever find his killers?"

"Yes, and they're after me now."

"Can't help you there," Doctor West said.

I looked at Goodnight and he shrugged his shoulders.

"There's several medicines we call AEDs to keep it under control. You have to stay on it for a while and the seizures might quit coming, but in the meantime you may have more. You may experience periods of unusual behavior: staring into space for no reason, leg and arms jerking, passing out. It's very serious, so take it serious, take the medicine and let me know if you have any more seizures. I'm going to start you off with Gahapentin. Less side effects and you can take it orally instead of an injection every day."

"Long as it works," I said. "I got some unfinished business to take care of."

"The nurse will bring you the medicine, follow the prescription. Call me after two or three days and let me know if it's working." He handed me a business card from his pocket.

"I will," I said.

"Good luck," he said.

Goodnight stood up walked over to the bed.

"You know that dog came to you like he knew something wasn't right."

"Yeah he did, didn't he. I pretended he was a therapy dog to get him on a flight. Maybe he is using canine instincts."

"Could be," Goodnight said.

"You need to take your medicine. Put Scooter in the bed with you and get some rest," Sandy said.

"I'm okay now," I said.

"I think she's right," Goodnight said. "You can crash in the guest room when we get back."

"Listen to us, Clark," Sandy said.

I nodded and smiled at Sandy.

After a four-hour nap, me and Scooter got up. Goodnight was on the phone with someone. Julie and Sandy were having a snack in the kitchen and the kids playing video games. Everything looked normal, but I knew it would be turned upside-down soon if I stayed.

It was time to leave.

I went back to the room, found a pen and paper and wrote a note explaining why I should leave and asked that they not make an attempt to call or find me. Told Sandy to entrust her safety with Goodnight and to put her money in a bank savings box, to find some unknown place to start her life over. And I asked Mary Ann to take care of Scooter. I sat the note on the end table, packed my medicine and Brandon's revolver in my bag and picked it up. I started to walk out the back door and I couldn't do it. I was being a coward. I should tell them eye-to-eye. I dropped the bag back on the bed and walked in the kitchen over to Sandy.

"I need to have a talk with you," I said.

"Me?" Sandy said.

"All of you. It's time for me to get out of your lives."

"And do what?" Sandy said. "I know you're not going to leave Junior out there."

"No, but the only way I can do that is without you and the

others being a target."

"I'm already a target. I'm up to my ass in this. I need you."

"I'm no better."

"You are to me," Sandy said.

"Do you know how to shoot a gun, Sandy?"

"Never have," she said.

"What I thought. Julie, do you?"

"Yes, I carry one all the time," she said.

"Would you teach Sandy?"

"Sure," Julie said.

"Sandy, with me gone, they may come after you. You need to know how to use a pistol. A revolver is the easiest to handle." I took Wiggins' Colt out of my belt. "You can see if it's loaded by looking at the back of the cylinder." I turned the Colt around so she could see the rounds. "If it's loaded—aim, squeeze the trigger. That's all there is to it. Julie will teach you how to load it."

"Sure," Julie said.

"Here, take Wiggins', I'll get another one," I said and handed her the Colt. "Put it in your purse."

Sandy took the Colt, frowned, dropped it in her purse.

I heard Sonny say bye to whoever he was on the phone with. He walked in the kitchen and looked at me.

"Did I hear you say you wanted to leave," he said.

"Yeah, time to go," I said.

"That would have made a lot of sense a year ago when I asked you to leave. It's a different thing now," Sonny said. "I know you thought what you did was the right thing to do. Now it's revenge on everyone's part. The time to investigate President Kennedy's murder is long gone. No one's left to do anything or punish the guilty, even if it was true."

"I'm still here," I said.

"Let it go and I'll find something I can charge Junior and Brandon with to put them in jail and you move on. Your Super Sport is in the garage. I haven't driven it since I took you to the airport."

"It's not mine, I sold it to you," I said. "I wanted you to have it."

"For a dollar, that ridiculous," Sonny said. "It's your car."

"I didn't think I was coming back," I said.

"Well here you are," he said. "Take it and you and Sandy get out of town."

"Let's load up and go," Sandy said.

"You stay here, I'll go," I said.

"You don't want me?"

"Leaving won't change anything. They'll find me and kill you and Mary Ann, too."

"I'm going," Sandy said. "Julie, would you watch after Mary Ann until we find us a place?"

"Sure," Julie said.

"I don't want you to go. You understand?"

"He's right, Sandy," Sonny said. "They would kill Mary Ann too if they got to you. No witnesses. Clark has a better chance if he don't have to worry about you and your daughter."

"Find you a place and a new name to start over, Sandy," I said. "Don't tell me or anyone else. If I don't know they can't make me tell them. I'm not worth the gamble."

Sandy started crying and ran out of the kitchen, Julie following.

Scooter sat at my feet looking at me. I glanced down at him.

"I better take my medicine," I said and went back to the guest room where I left my bag. I took my medicine, walked back in the kitchen and Sonny pitched me the keys to the Super Sport. "Forget the Colt. I don't know about it."

"Thanks," I said. "Watch over Sandy and Mary Ann for me. I gave her all the money she will ever need. Help her find a place far away from here. Mary Ann can keep Scooter."

I picked up my bag in the guest room and walked out to the garage to the Super Sport, Sonny following me.

"If I don't make it back, put me in a grave beside my wife and son. You can have the Super Sport and anything else I got you want."

"You'll make it," Sonny said. "You're one of the best and bravest warriors I ever saw."

"We'll see." I opened the car door, pitched the bag in, cranked it and rolled the window down to shake hands.

"Thanks," I said. "Tell Sandy I'm sorry, but this is best for her and her baby."

"You know she loves you," Sonny said.

"I love her in my own way, too, but she has a future. I don't. I'm too old for her."

Sonny nodded, opened the garage door with the remote and I backed the Super Sport out and drove away.

I had a feeling of relief. Sandy and Mary Ann were better off.

Two blocks away, Pepper called.

"Brandon Twotrees busted in my place, shooting it up. I got to my car, barely escaped," she said. "Where are you?"

"I'm in D.C. Anyone following you?"

"I don't know. I'm on Thirty-Fourth Street headed north," she said. "In a red BMW."

"I'm in the Super Sport. Stop at the Broadway parking garage. Park on the street. I'll be there in about fifteen minutes."

"Me too," she said. "No one's crowding me."

"You got a weapon?"

"Yeah, my nine-millimeter."

"Keep it ready. I'll be there soon. Don't call the cops."

5

I ran a caution light in the next block and hauled ass down the street for about five more blocks and saw her red BMW parked in front of the Broadway Parking Garage on the other side of the street. Their red white and blue neon sign flashing with an arrow pointing to the inside. I ran past her, made a one-eighty after a delivery truck went by and pulled up behind her. There weren't any cars parked nearby with anyone in them. I called Pepper. She said, "I see you Clark."

"Put your phone on speaker, hit the gas and let me know which way you're turning on the street before you get there. I'll watch for company. If there's nothing after a couple of miles, find a side street and we'll stop and make a plan to outfox these bastards."

"Where's Sandy?" she said.

"At Goodnight's. I'm going to leave her there."

"Sounds like a good idea. Hang on to your hat. I think My BMW can outrun you. I'll keep you in sight."

"I don't think so. Hammer down and we'll find out. If the police show up keep going. I'll distract them."

"Phone's on speaker. Here we go," she said.

We whizzed down the street, constantly checking the rearview mirror, weaving in and out of traffic, drivers and pedestrians staring at us like we were crazy. Unfortunately, I may be, I thought. I saw a toll gate coming up and talked to my phone.

"Turn right on the next street," I said.

"Gotcha," Pepper said.

The brake light came on and she made a sharp turn and straightened up and drove into a fast food parking lot to a parking space in the back. I parked beside her. We left the cars running, waiting to see if anyone was after us. Five minutes later we cut the engines. I stuck the Colt back under my shirt and walked up to Pepper's car. She unlocked it and I got in. She leaned over an hugged me and I hugged her back.

"Thank god you're alive," she said.

"Somewhat. I have epilepsy from the Trilene. Taking pills. Working so far. What happened between you and Matt?"

"He wanted to get married and I didn't. Our war's not over with the Parkers. You need me."

"Oh no. I want you to make up with Matt." I could see the fire in her beautiful brown eyes. She wasn't kidding, she wanted revenge.

"They murdered my parents and brother and tried to murder you. As a lawyer, I filed a complaint for an arrest warrant but it was thrown out for lack of evidence by one of their judges. We're past getting anything done by the law."

"Amanda—," I said and she interrupted.

"That means you want me to do something you know I don't want to do. That's what my daddy always said when we were at odds over something. Who saved your ass at the Parker mansion?"

"You keep reminding me of that. I don't want you to have to do it again. It may not work out right next time."

"I'm a trained special operations soldier like you. I've been in combat. We both know they will come after us until we're dead or they are. I prefer the latter. You were my brother's godfather. Aren't you mine, too?"

"Of course. That's why you should make up with Matt. Find a new life."

"If something happened to you and I could have been there to help and wasn't," she said, hesitating, "I would feel guilty the rest of my life. You and my dad had a special bond. You proved it to each other time and time again. I love you and believe in you. I know what I'm getting into."

"He saved my life when we were under fire in Vietnam. That's what I was trying to do for you—take you out of harm's way—but I can see that's not going to work."

"Nope," she said. "We're in this together. To the end. Whatever that is. You know there's no in-between. It's us or them. Those bastards deserve to die."

"Got kind of a mean streak yourself, don't you," I said.

"When I need it. They wiped out my family—"

The back window exploded.

Bullets passed by my head out the windshield on my side. Pepper ducked down. I laid down in the seat, put my left hand on Pepper to hold her down and opened the car door with my other hand. The windshield crumbled, throwing glass in the seat, leaving small cuts on our hands. Pepper drew her nine-millimeter from a thigh holster. I slid out of the car to the pavement, pulling Pepper out behind me. With a peek under the car, I saw a Mercedes in the alley across the street from us, a rifle sticking out a half-opened back window.

"They're shooting from the alley," I yelled at Pepper. "Get against the wheel." I slid over to the front tire. "Are you okay?"

"Yes," she said.

"Stay down."

Seconds later, another volley of automatic weapon fire hit

the side of the car. The tires went flat, bullets bouncing under the car, missing us by inches. We heard people screaming as they ran away. Another round of bullets set the car engine on fire. The fire would reach the gas tank in seconds and explode. We had to make a run.

We jumped up, hauling ass away from the car and heard a siren in the distance. The shooter's car peeled out of the alley — too fast to get the license plate number.

I looked up and saw a door to the building in front of us about twenty yards away. I pointed at the door. Pepper nodded, put her automatic back in the thigh holster. I stuck the Colt in my belt. We made a beeline to the door. Just as we opened it the car exploded, pieces bouncing off the building wall. The sound of the siren was fading. It wasn't coming for us. We peeked out the door. My Super Sport looked like Swiss cheese, with a part of Pepper's car hood sitting on top of it, still burning.

"Holy hell. They destroyed both our cars," I said.

"You think that's it?" Pepper said.

"For now. Where are we?" I looked around. We were in a hamburger joint. "You hungry?" She nodded yes.

We walked up to the counter. Three people were laying on the floor behind it. I leaned over the counter. "We called 911, they're on the way. The bad guys are gone. We want to order."

They got up and went back to work. A teenage girl moved to the register.

"What will you have," she said.

I looked up at the menu. "Number five and a large Coke," I said.

"Me too," Pepper said.

A few minutes later we picked up our lunch and walked over to a table.

"I'll get the drinks," I said.

A little man with a manger tag on his shirt walked up to our table.

"Get out of my store," he said.

"We will when the police get here," Pepper said. "You see

what happened to our cars? We don't have any transportation."

I nodded and took a bite of my hamburger.

"You going to call Goodnight?" Pepper said.

"As soon as I finish eating and take my epileptic pill," I said.

"Is he going to have a fit?" The manager asked.

"Could," Pepper said, and smiled at me.

The manager's eyes got big and he walked away, dialing his phone.

6

"Thanks for coming to get us, Sonny," I said and sat down next to Pepper in Sonny Goodnight's office. The certificates and valor awards were still on the walls and the silver-framed picture of his wife and kids on his desk.

"The restaurant wants to sue you," he said.

"We were attacked in the parking lot. What the hell were we supposed to do?" I said. "A wrecker hauled the cars away."

"I don't know. Pepper, that's in your wheel house."

"I'll deal with it later," Pepper said.

"You at least know who it was?" Goodnight said.

"I could guess but it all happened so fast we were lucky to make it out alive," I said.

"Did you see the tag?" Goodnight asked.

"No. They were firing from a black Mercedes in an alley

across the street so fast we had to stay put," Pepper said. "They hauled ass when they heard sirens blocks away but they weren't coming to us. I called 911 from the restaurant and the police and a fire engine showed up in about fifteen minutes. They put the car fires out. I signed a report for the cops."

"I don't think I can fix the Super Sport this time," I said. "Not only is it full of holes but the fire department drowned it, too."

"Yeah it's dead. Miracle you're not," Sonny said.

"How's Sandy and Mary Ann?" I said.

"She's pissed off at you big time. Said she's going to give you back the money and go back to Long Shore. What money?"

"She can't do that, they would kill her," I said. "It's money Robert had in a Swiss bank account that I had a power of attorney for. Me and Pepper didn't want so I gave it to Sandy. Take us to a car rental. I'll pick up Sandy and Mary Ann. We got to get out of your house as soon as we can."

"If she will go. She's really upset," Goodnight said.

"Get you a rental and take me to a BMW dealer," Pepper said. "We can all go to my house. I need a bath."

"Me, too, but don't think that will work. They're probably waiting for us there. We can clean up at Goodnight's and get out of his house."

"You going to force Sandy to go?" Pepper asked.

"If I have to."

"I think you do need to leave the house," Sonny said. "Afraid someone will shoot my family and I don't want to be a witness to a kidnapping if you force Sandy to go with you."

"I'll work it out with her," I said.

"I think Matt can find us a safe place to stay for a day or two," Pepper said.

Goodnight dropped us off at the car rental and I drove Pepper to a BMW dealer where she leased a car and followed me to Goodnight's. I called Goodnight and told him I was going to pick up Sandy and Mary Ann and leave before someone shot up his house.

When we walked in, Sandy was watching the news but got

up and left the room.

Pepper rolled her eyes and shook her head. "You're in trouble," she said.

I sighed and went looking for Sandy. She was in the kitchen, pouring Mary Ann a glass of milk. She gave me a go-to-hell look and left the kitchen. I heard Julie and the boys in another room talking and followed Sandy to the bedroom, she closed the door and locked it before I could get to it. I had to talk to her through the door.

"I'm sorry," I said. "I was trying to protect you, not abandoned you. We have to get out of Goodnight's house. They tried to kill me and Pepper this morning."

I heard the lock on the door snap unlocked and stood in the doorway.

"You and Pepper should get as far away from here as you can," she said. "I'm going back to Long Shore and I want you to take the money back."

"Look, I made a mistake. I'm sorry. I thought you would be in more danger with me. You can't go back to Long Shore, they would kill you and your baby as soon as they found out you were there."

"I'm a burden to you," she said.

"No you're not. Pack your bag, we have to get out of Goodnight's house before they show up and riddle it with bullets."

"Okay." She nodded as a tear ran down her cheek. She put her arms around me and I hugged her and kissed her on the cheek.

"I'll get Mary Ann," she said. "We'll be ready in a few minutes. Where we going?"

"I don't know yet but we have to go now."

"I won't be long," she said.

I walked back to the living room to say goodbye to Goodnight and his family. All hell was going to break loose soon. I reached in Sandy's purse on the table, grabbed the Colt and stuck it back in my belt.

I need more guns, I thought.

I got a call from Goodnight. He thanked me for leaving the house with Sandy and asked me to keep him informed and he would try to help. It was a good feeling to know we went from enemies to friends.

Pepper called Matt and he found us a safe house. I could tell by the conversation they were still in love. She trusted him, so did I.

Pepper wanted to bring her car too. We parked both cars in a church parking lot as instructed. Matt arrived a few minutes later, waved at us to follow and we did. He turned on a small street named Sylvia and stopped at a gated apartment building. The gate opened and we followed him in. He parked and got out of his car so we did the same. Pepper hugged him. He rushed us into a small apartment in the middle of a long apartment building, stuck out his hand to shake and smiled at me. I shook his hand and smiled back.

He unlocked apartment 109. We went in. Nothing suspicious looking.

"Good to see you, Clark," he said.

"You too, Matt," I said.

"Who's the woman and girl?" he asked.

"Someone I have to take care of. She got involved by accident. We can trust her."

"I'll set up some watch patrols for the next twenty-four hours. This should do for tonight. I know the FBI is checking out the file you sent them. Probably too late to do anything now. Elton Junior is trying to get something on you to send you to jail or kill you, whichever comes first. I've been talking to the FBI about that but all they want is to get rid of you. Don't think they would make a deal with you."

"That doesn't surprise me. You and Pepper working things out?"

"I think so," he said.

"I tried to get her to let me handle this on my own. She wouldn't listen," I said.

"I know. She can be hard-headed when she thinks she's right," Matt said.

"Gets it naturally. Her daddy was the same way. I'll try to think of something to get her back to you."

"Thanks, there's food, water and drinks in the fridge. The attic door in the hall goes into an empty apartment next door for an escape route. Don't go out until tomorrow. If anyone comes to the door for a normal reason, Alvin Smith lives here. That's the name on the mailbox. Gate code is seven-two-three-three."

"Thanks again, Matt."

"You bet." He handed me the door keys and walked over to Pepper. They hugged and kissed. He introduced himself to Sandy, said goodbye and left.

I locked the door behind him. I could see a bedroom down a hall from an open door and a small kitchen off the other side of the room with a stove and refrigerator. The girls could pile in the bedroom bed and I would camp on the couch. The only bathroom had to be in the bedroom. I noticed a large stain on the carpet by the back door. Someone may have died here. This was not the kind of place you could put much confidence in.

Sandy walked over to me. "Pepper said her boyfriend's a spy."

"He's in the Army intelligence, a major," I said.

"Maybe he can help us get out of this mess," she said.

"Not much he can legally do." My hands began to tremble. "I got to take a pill," I said.

Mary Ann came up to me.

"Are we going to stay here, Mr. Clark?" she said.

I didn't like that name either. Still too formal.

"Not for very long. We'll find us a good place soon."

She nodded, didn't say anything and walked away.

"I'll get you water," she said and headed for the kitchenette.

I reached in my pocket, got the medicine bottle and had to hold on with both my shaking hands to open it. I started drooling and getting dizzy. Sandy came back with the water. I spilled some but managed to take the pill and was feeling better in the next thirty minutes.

We found TV dinners to eat, then the girls took a shower and dressed in clean clothes they brought and laid down on the floor watching television. It had been a long day. I slipped off my shoes and stretched out on the couch. I didn't want to get caught naked again. I'll take a shower in the morning, I thought to myself.

About two hours later, the girls went to the bedroom. I laid Wiggins' Colt beside me with the trigger guard turned to me. It was an uneasy night as cars came in and out of the gate all night. The two pistols we had wouldn't be enough if they came after us. I had to come up with a plan to get Pepper and Sandy out of this, I could never forgive myself if something happened to them.

I dozed off to sleep around midnight, a few Vietnam dreams flickering through my head, causing me to wake up several times. I gave it up about five, got up, put my shoes on and found coffee in the cabinet. The girls were still asleep and didn't drink coffee but us dinosaurs did and acquired the habit at an early age. We didn't always have all the fancy drinks they have now. Leaning up against a cabinet waiting for the coffee, looking around the hiding place, I realized we needed more freedom of movement and a better way out.

That wasn't the only thing I was thinking about. Maybe it wouldn't have been this way if I had just went to the funerals and back to Texas. But I couldn't bring myself to do that knowing someone murdered my best friend and his wife, then their son, and the cops or his employer the CIA not giving a damn. I found the killers but they were still coming after me and it was forcing innocent people to go through hell with me.

I poured a cup of coffee, turned the television on without sound and sat down on the couch. Text ran across the screen saying Elton Parker Junior, a New York congressional representative, was shot dead in his New York office yesterday. Found by staff members. FBI investigating.

The cup fell out of my hand, the hot coffee burning my fingers as it crashed to the floor. The sound of the breaking cup woke the girls.

"What happened?" Pepper said, running in rubbing her eyes. "Someone in the house?"

"No, Junior Parker is dead. He was murdered. It's on TV."

"Do they know who did it?" Pepper asked, sitting down on the couch.

"They don't, but I think I do. It was Brandon. The old man gave everything to Junior except the mansion and Brandon burned it down. They never got along before the old man died and Parker never included Brandon in anything except when he wanted him to do something no one else would."

"This may mean our troubles are over," Sandy said.

"No, it will get worse now," I said. "Brandon is too stupid to plan anything. He just reacts without thinking. He still remembers the whipping I gave him and, without Junior to control him, I think he will come after me when he knows I'm back in the states."

"I think the CIA did it," Pepper said. "Crooked agents Carter and Martinez were pissed off because he couldn't kill you and they were afraid you would testify to what you saw in my daddy's CIA file about the JFK conspiracy."

"I have to do this on my own. I know an old dude that works at the Majestic Hotel where I think can help get more firepower and keep you two out of this."

"That's a bad place. You go there they'll strip your car and kill you," Pepper said.

"Look, I have to do what I have to do."

7

I ventured out the gate the next morning and parked in a department store parking lot. Once I was sure I wasn't followed, I called a taxi and waited.

The taxi driver showed up about fifteen minutes later. I got in, but when I told him where I wanted to go he put the meter handle back up and waved his arm for me to get out.

"I'll double the fare if you take me," I said. "You can drop me off and leave. I'm going to be there for a while."

"For a while. More like forever," he moved his hands in a prayer position.

"I'll pay double," I said. "Take me there, let me out and you can high-tail it out of there."

I glanced at his name tag. His name was Espar.

"I'll pay you double again to come get me when I'm ready,

Espar. You won't have to wait."

"Bad place," he said.

He held out his hand for the money. "Sixty-four dollars."

I counted out the money and handed it to him. He counted it and we headed for the Majestic Hotel.

As we got closer to the hotel there were more dirty streets, drug dealers and street girls. Only way they had making a living there, I thought. He stopped in front of the hotel and two kids stopped shooting baskets at a basketball rim attached to a brick wall in an abandoned parking lot across the street. A large mural of life on the street was painted on the brick building wall. The one holding the basketball put it under his arm and they both started walking toward the taxi. I barely had time to close the taxi door before Espar took off.

I turned to the hotel. The graffiti plastered all over the front of the hotel was still there. A pile of garbage was no more than a half a block away, rats still having a fiesta. The two kids crossed the street. Both of them wearing basketball shorts and plain black sleeveless shirts.

I pushed the dilapidated revolving door around and walked in the hotel. Gizmo was sitting on his stool in the cage stroking a black Persian cat, looking at something on the counter. It hadn't been long since I was here, he may remember me, I thought.

The kids stopped at the hotel door and walked away. I was in Gizmo's territory now. He heard my steps, quit stroking the cat and looked up at me.

"I'll be damned, if it ain't Mister Not Important." He pushed his Nationals baseball cap back on his head, his curly gray hair sticking out the sides. He still had his short salt-and-pepper beard. The cat jumped down from the counter and disappeared.

"I need help," I said.

"You ain't going to find it here," Gizmo said. "Nobody gives a shit about anyone except themself." The cat jumped back up on the counter.

"Only friend I got is Sissy here," he said and started stroking her again.

"I need guns," I said.

"Guns. I'm still wondering what happened to that Barbawitz guy you came here after?"

"Tried to kill me, had to kill him first," I said.

"You don't take no shit, do you?"

"Nope."

We heard the hotel door spin and looked at the door. I checked my belt for the Colt. A pretty young black girl wearing a revealing red dress and spike high heels made a drum tap on the floor as she approached the cage.

It was always like an alarm for Gizmo. It meant money. A working girl had arrived. She looked my way and smiled.

Gizmo waved his hand at her. "He's looking for something else," Gizmo said. "You early today, Tristen." He handed her a key and she gave it back to him.

"Not working today, Gizmo." She looked at me and smiled again. "Unless it's something special. You need some company, mister?"

"He wants guns," Gizmo said.

"Guns? You a cop, mister?"

"You think he would tell you? He's not," Gizmo said. "Mister Not Important has been here before." Gizmo turned to me. "Tristen probably knows where you can get guns."

"I want an AR-15, two .45s, two .357 revolvers and a hundred rounds for each, no questions asked."

"You got cash," Tristen said.

"You think I'm stupid? You have a bank account?"

"No."

"I got one," Gizmo said. "I'll keep five hundred and give Tristen whatever she says if you send it."

"If I can find what you want it will be four thousand plus five hundred apiece for me and Gizmo. You got that kind of money?"

"You've done this before, haven't you?" I said.

"None of your business. You said no questions," Tristen said.

"I got the money," I said.

"Good," she said. "Stay put. I'll be back in a couple of hours. You better be telling the truth or you'll never leave here alive."

"You don't need to threaten me. This isn't a sting," I said. "I'll be here."

Tristen turned away and walked out of the hotel. The two kids were still standing outside the hotel door.

"Might be better if you get out of view from the front, Mister Not Important, kind of tempting the boys to come after you," Gizmo said.

I moved away from the door but stayed inside in view of it, waiting for Tristen.

A little over two hours later, she came in carrying a bag and sat it on the floor beside the cage.

"That's all I could get now. Take it or leave it."

I unzipped the bag and checked the contents. A .45, a .357 revolver and three boxes of shells.

"Well, I need what I can get," I said. "How much? I'll wire the money."

Gizmo handed me a canceled check.

"Give you a discount," Tristen said and smiled. "Two thousand for the guns, five hundred for the ammo and five hundred a piece for me and Gizmo. You wait here until Gizmo gives me my money."

"I'll make the call and they'll send the money," I said.

"Mister, I'm sure you know Tristen is my working name not my real one, and this is going to be my last day at the hotel. Don't ever try to get in touch with me."

I nodded. The money came in and Gizmo counted out cash to Tristen from the safe.

"I don't need you no more either, Gizmo," she said and headed for the hotel door. We watched her walk out and disappear on the sidewalk.

"Damn, she was one of my best girls," Gizmo said.

The cat jumped back up on the counter and Gizmo started stroking her again.

"Think it's time for you to leave, Mister Not Important,"

Gizmo said.

"You're right, Gizmo. Take care of your pussy."

"I always do," Gizmo said.

I dialed the taxi and waited inside until he pulled up to the curb. Gizmo dropped his cat on the floor and hobbled out of the cage to the door with his cane. He opened the taxi door and I got in with my bag. The two kids started walking toward the cab from across the street.

"Good luck Mister Not Important," he said. "Don't come back."

"I won't."

He closed the taxi door and the cab sped away.

"You paying double, that right?" the taxi driver said.

"Yeah," I said. "Where's Espar?"

"Not coming, sent me and said you pay double?" he said as we hauled ass from the Majestic.

"The Wal-Mart parking lot on Hudson," I said.

"I know where it is," he said.

He pulled the bill down a little on his Yankee baseball cap and rubbed his black goatee with the back of his hand. I couldn't make out his name on the cab ID card. Had a dozen letters in it. He drove in the Wal-Mart parking lot about thirty minutes later and I pointed out my car.

"Going to be seventy-four dollars," he said as he stopped beside my car. I shook my head at the increase, counted out the money and handed it to him over the seat.

He reached back and took it. I got out of the taxi, sat the bag in the back seat, got in and headed for the apartment.

On my way, Goodnight called to let me know that the FBI said the murder of Parker Junior would shut down the file on Elton Parker and the JFK conspiracy file would be returned to the CIA and classified to stop any further inquiries into it. Been too long to open another investigation. Would be better for me to leave Washington immediately.

"I think they're right," Goodnight said.

"I can get you in the witness protection program, give you

and Sandy new names and all that. Someplace Brandon and his cronies won't look."

"Set something up for Sandy and her kid. I'll do what I have to do."

"You better rethink it, no need for you to spend the rest of your life in prison," he said.

"To late for forgiveness, for me or them. It's last man standing. I'm young enough to live, old enough to die. We wouldn't be talking about this if I had not got you and the girls in it. Time for me to finish it."

"You're wrong, Clark, it would have happened either way. Regrets are only good when you don't have any other options, and you do," he said and hung up.

When I got to the apartment I carried the bag in, sat it down on the floor and told Sandy and Pepper what Goodnight said.

"Pepper, you go to Matt and find you a future. You're on the wrong track with me. Sandy, you and Mary Ann can stay with me until Goodnight finds you a better place."

"Where we going," Sandy said.

"To pick up Scooter then leave town. Beyond that, I don't know yet." I took the Colt from my belt and handed it to Sandy. "I borrowed this. You can have it back now."

"I never knew it was gone," she said.

"Remember it from now on. Never know when you might need it."

I reached down, picked up the bag, sat it on the table and took out the weapons, loading and strapping them on, sharing the ammo with Sandy.

"Keep this in your purse," I said. She took the boxes and put them in her purse.

"I'll go with you," Pepper said.

"No, go to Matt. I'll be in touch."

"You sure you're doing the right thing?" Pepper said. "I'm your good girl."

"You are, but I think I can handle it. If I can't, I'll count on you to bury me."

"I'm ready if you change your mind," Pepper said.

"I know, you always are. Bye for now." I hung up and put the phone back in my pocket. "Sandy, we got to go."

"I'll get my things," Sandy said.

After we picked up Scooter and said goodbye to Julie and the boys, I got to thinking about our dilemma. I called Pepper.

"We're on our way out of D.C.," I said. "Go to Matt, I know your daddy would tell you the same thing. We'll be alright."

"You've always been like another father to me. You might not think I listen but I do. Matt is on his way here. He's been transferred to Europe. I'm going with him. If it's alright with you."

"That's what I want you to do," I said.

"Clark, I owe you. You made them pay for murdering my family," Pepper said.

"No you don't. You're a special person that should have a special life," I said and hung up.

I looked at Sandy. I could see how frightened she was.

"We'll come out of this the winners, Sandy, as long as we think we will."

"I'm afraid for my baby more than anything," she said.

I nodded in agreement and looked in the back seat. Mary Ann and Scooter were snuggled up to each other asleep.

"If we split up you got no one else to protect her. They have to get through me first and that's not going to happen. The FBI and CIA backed off. It's Wiggins and Brandon we have to watch for. Wiggins and Brandon will show up sooner or later. Wiggins is after money and Brandon hates my guts. It's too late to correct the past. We have to concentrate on the present."

"What are you going to do," Sandy said

"If they come they won't leave," I said. "If they don't, I'll leave them alone."

"Don't you have some friends in Texas that could help us?"

"I do but I don't want to do the same thing to them that I have to you and Pepper. Too late to change that now, but I can save someone else from the trouble."

8

We stopped for the night at a small motel under a false name. They didn't ask for ID but may have taken the licenses plate number from my rental. It said no pets on the office door but I sneaked Scooter in anyway.

Later that night, I got a headache and stumbled into the bathroom. The room started spinning. I slid down to the floor. Took a pill and my head cleared up so I went back to bed.

The next morning, we ate breakfast and fed Scooter in the car. I took my prescription bottle to a pharmacy for a refill but they wouldn't refill it because it didn't have a refill on the bottle. I was down to two pills.

"Call your doctor," Sandy said. "You got to have pills."

"We'll find a pharmacy in the next town. I'll call."

As we pulled into the next town in Arkansas, I saw a for sale sign on a seventy-three SS sitting next to a house. Wasn't as good as the one I had but it looked pretty good, and I knew it had a big engine and could run like hell. I slowed down and drove into the driveway.

"You don't want that do you?" Sandy said.

"Maybe," I said.

"We need a good car," Sandy said.

"That is a good car, can outrun 'em." I got out and left the car running.

An old man, older than me, opened the front door of his house and walked out. He had white hair and matching whiskers, wearing overalls. I noticed his hands looked calloused and he had large biceps, might be a mechanic.

"What you want for it?" I asked.

"Need to sell it. Give you a good price. In good shape. I rebuilt it last year."

So he was a mechanic, I thought to myself.

"Twenty-thou cash, got a title," he said.

Sandy was looking at me out the car window, shaking her head no. He saw her shaking her head.

"Women never appreciate cars," he said.

"Nope," I said, "but I guess she's right. We need a more ordinary ride. Think I'll pass, sorry for bothering you."

"Change your mind, I'll be here," he said.

I got back in the car and drove away. I didn't say anything and she didn't say anything. She just smiled, giving me her approval for not buying the car.

We located a pharmacy. I called Doctor West but no answer. I waited an hour and called two more times before anyone answered. To my surprise it was Goodnight.

"What are you doing there?" I said.

"Someone killed Doctor West," Goodnight said. "His nurse found him dead in his office this morning. He had been beaten up before he was shot. May have been the Parkers looking for you, thinking he knew where you were."

"Killing West is the last straw," I said.

"You could be tried for murder if you go after them," Goodnight said.

"Don't worry about me. Find Sandy a place," I said.

"You're not thinking clear. I have the nurse's private number. Call her and she can send you the prescription. You better rethink what you're going to do."

"Don't want to talk about it anymore. Give me the number." I took my phone out of my pocket. He did and I punched it in my phone for a later call. "You're a good man, Sonny. Find a safe place for Sandy and Mary Ann. It's the last thing I'll ask you to do, friend."

"I'll come up with something as soon as I can. Keep moving for now," he said.

"It's my son's birthday. We're getting close to Brookville. I'm going to make a run by the graveyard and then move on," I said.

"Don't stay long," he said.

"We won't." I hung up, laid my phone on my lap and looked at Sandy with a big sigh. "He said Doctor West was murdered. Must have thought he knew where we were."

"I don't want to leave you," she leaned over and kissed me on the cheek.

"You may not have to," I said.

A little while later, I saw a pharmacy sign so I pulled into a parking lot in Texarkana just across the border in Texas. Made contact with Doctor West's nurse and she called in the prescription. I picked up the medicine and headed to Brookville. a town I grew up in.

I wanted to visit the graves one more time before I joined them. Especially on Cooper's birthday. Didn't tell Sandy that her ex and Brandon may already be waiting for us.

As I drove into Brookville, I noticed the old movie house was still open. Spent a lot of time there as a kid, I remembered. Next was Wendell Moore's law firm. We still talked on the phone now and then about my legal problems. And somehow always wound up talking about high school and football. And then the First State Bank where my money was handled by my old friend

Dewey Reynolds.

I drove on across town, turned off on the cemetery road, drove through the open gate to the graves of my family. A four-foot iron fence surrounded the graves, with a space for one more—that would be me.

I thought about how Billie had told me she wanted to be buried in France with her family.

We got out of the car, Scooter peed on a grave. Thank goodness no one saw him.

We walked up to Mary's and Cooper's graves. I stood there looking at them with memories racing through my mind.

Like the last time I saw Mary alive.

She walked in the kitchen that day for the last time when I was pouring a glass of orange juice. I picked the keys off the hook as she was telling me to pick up pizza for dinner later that night. She headed out the door to go pick up Cooper. I heard the door close and then open again. She walked back in the kitchen smiling.

"Something told me to say goodbye again," she said and hugged my neck and kissed me. "I love you."

"I love you, too," I said as she smiled again and walked away for the last time.

And like that, I was back in the real world.

"We're going to get back in the car, Clark, so you can have some privacy with your loved ones."

I nodded and kneeled down, Scooter laid down beside me. Sandy took May's hand and they walked back to the car.

"Mary, I miss you and Cooper every day. You're always on my mind. I was poisoned. Getting worse. Have a lady, her daughter and a dog depending on me for survival. Only thing that keeps me going. Wanted you and Cooper to know. I love you. I may join you at anytime. Bye for now."

I stood up, Scooter got up. We walked back to the car.

I took one last look and drove away.

9

As I drove through town I kept my eyes peeled for D.C. license plates. Didn't see any. It occurred to me this would be a good time to move Sandy's bank account to my bank. My lifelong friend and banker Dewy Reynolds could come up with legal ways to delay Wiggins' withdrawal and contact Sandy. I could also check my bank box for the picture albums, my medals, letters and other items I put in it when Mary and Cooper died.

"Sandy, the guy that runs the bank is is a good friend of mine. He can figure out legal ways to keep Wiggins from getting it. Let's go see him."

"Fine with me," she said.

We parked in front of the bank, Scooter started barking. He knew what was happening. He would have to stay in the car again.

When we walked in, I saw Dewey in a glass office with President on the door. He was by himself. I motioned for Sandy and Mary Ann to sit down then walked up to his receptionist's desk.

"I'd like to see Dewey, please," I said.

Her glasses were pushed down on her nose. She pushed them back up, staring at me. Her gray eyes matched her hair she had in a bun.

"Are you Clark McKay?" she said and smiled.

"Yes," I said. "I thought I knew you."

"Roberta Young," she said. "They call me Robby. I was a friend of your high school girlfriend Janet Selman."

"Yeah, of course. Where's Janet these day?"

"She went to college and never came back. I married your friend Roy Peterson."

"You two still married?"

"Yep, we got two boys in college."

"That's great," I said.

"I'll get Mr. Reynolds." She opened Dewey's office door, he was looking at a file on his desk.

"Look who's here," she said. Dewey looked up.

"Well I'll be damned," he said.

We shook hands and he invited me to his office. I waved at Sandy and Mary Ann. They got up and we followed him in and we sat down, Dewey standing behind his desk.

"Clark, I do a lot of business for you but I haven't seen you in years. How are you doing?"

"Not too sure. We just got in town. I need you to take care of some things."

"Sure, whatever you need."

"This is Sandy Wiggins, Dewey," I said.

He nodded at Sandy and smiled.

"Can I close the door?" I said.

"I got it," Robby said and closed it as she walked out.

"Must be important for you to do it in person," he said.

"It is and it's also important that you don't tell anyone."

"Only the bank examiners," he said and grinned.

"I know you're going to think this is a little strange," I said. "I inherited two million dollars from a deceased 'Nam buddy's bank account in Switzerland. It was dirty money, but legal. Sandy needed help and since I didn't want it I gave it to her. It's in a bank in Long Shore, New York in her name. She didn't get a divorce from her ex when he left before I gave her the money. If he finds out she's got that much money he's going to come after it. He's still her legal husband."

"That's a lot of money. What you want me to do?" Dewey said.

"Find a legal way to keep it out of his reach," I said.

"The easiest way would be to have her give it back to you, put it in your bank account, set up a smaller one in her name, then transfer money from the big account to the smaller one as needed. Nothing he could do about the big money except file a claim that may never get to court."

"What if something happens to me?" I said.

"Sign a document giving her the money as inheritance. Leave it in your account. I'll loan her money with the inheritance as collateral as she needs it. Have Wendell fix up an inheritance document. I'll put it on file, that should do it."

"Beats what we got now. How does that sound to you, Sandy?"

"Sounds good to me. Do it," she said.

"Okay, Dewey, Sandy will give you the account number to transfer the money. I'll go see Wendell for the other part when we're done here."

"Come with me, Sandy," Dewey said and opened the door.

"I'll wait for you and we'll go see my lawyer."

Sandy nodded and they walked out of Dewey's office to another office, went in and closed the door. I sat down and waited.

A lot of old memories from my boyhood ran through my mind. The good and bad. Most were good.

Thirty minutes later, Sandy, Dewey and Mary Ann came out

of the office with a young man I didn't know. He shook hands with Sandy and she came over to me.

"I'll take care of it and keep doing what you want me to do with your money," Dewey said. "I was a little surprised by your request to send money to the Majestic Hotel in D.C. but you put your code on it so I sent it."

"Yeah. Was the right thing to do. As long it has my code on it you'll know it's okay."

"Has worked good," Dewey said. "You going to stay in town?"

"Don't know yet," I said.

"Okay, make sure I get the inheritance document."

"I'm going to see Garrett now."

"It was good to see you again. I missed you," Dewey said.

"I missed you too," I said.

We walked out of the bank and got in the car and Scooter went nuts jumping back and forth from the back seat to the front seat, licking everyone's face. I think he thought we were not coming back.

I drove down the street three blocks, parked in front of Garrett's office. Scooter was getting that strange look again, he knew what was going to happen. We got out, Scooter stuck his nose against the window looking at us, probably going to pee in the car out of spite.

We walked in and saw local pictures hanging on all the walls. Homecoming queens, one I knew. Football pictures, sports award pictures and in a corner by Wendell's office, pictures of him, his wife and kids, and two of me and Wendell celebrating a state football championship.

The lady at the front desk had a name plate on her desk that said Lucy Bowman.

"Can I help you," she said. I remembered the last name but I didn't know her. She must have married one of the Bowman boys. She looked to be about Sandy's age, maybe a little heavier, brown hair tied back in a ponytail with big round gold rings hanging from her ears. Two other women at a desk behind her glanced at us and went back to work. A closed office door off to the left from them with Garrett More - Attorney on one and Bill Johnson - Attorney on the other closed door.

"Is Garrett in?" I said.

"He's on the phone right now," she said, looking at a phone light on her desk The phone light went off.

"He's off the phone. What's your name, sir?"

"Clark McKay, we're old friends."

As if on cue, Garrett's office door opened He saw me. He didn't look his age. He still had a full head of neatly-trimmed black hair, slim, wearing a black suit, white shirt and red tie. He looked like he could still play quarterback. He ran back in his office, picked up a football and came running out again, waving his hand holding the football.

"Go long," he said and threw the football to me. I reached out and caught it. He raised his arms, "Touchdown!" The women were looking at us like we went crazy, including Sandy.

"You still got it." He ran up to me and put me in a bear hug.

I hugged him back, I was getting a little embarrassed with the ladies giving us strange looks.

"That winning catch you made in the state playoffs was spectacular," he said.

"If you hadn't escaped the rush and threw the ball nothing else would have happened."

"Yeah," he said. "Where the hell you been all these years? If you hadn't been calling me for legal things I would have thought you were dead. You come back to stay?"

"Don't know yet," I said.

"Who's this pretty lady you have with you?"

"Sandy Wiggins and her daughter Mary Ann," I said.

"It's a pleasure to meet you," Garrett said.

"I need to talk to you," I said.

"Give me my ball back and come on in my office and we'll talk. Would you like something to drink?"

We all shook our heads no and followed him in his office. He sat down at his desk and motioned for us to be seated and we did.

"Okay," he said. "What's up? You got more problems with the Parkers and Feds?"

"That situation's a lot better than it was but some scumbags are still trying to kill me."

"Evil always tries to harm the good," he said and grinned.

"I don't know about that but I need you to prepare an inheritance document giving Sandy two million dollars from my bank account that we transferred from her bank account to protect it from her ex, the one she's never got a divorce from."

"What kind of provisions do you want in it?" Garrett said.

"None. When I die she inherits the money, no catches. Give Dewey the document as soon as you get it done. He has worked out a plan to protect it for her and see that she has money now."

"If that's what you want," he said. "I'll need some information from Sandy and you to sign some papers."

"I'll sign them and you can fill them out later."

Garrett picked up two sheets of blank computer papers, marked a small X where he wanted me to sign and handed me a pen. I signed them and handed them back to him.

"I have some things we need to discuss about your house," he said. "We've been leasing it like you said with a maintenance clause but it needs some repair from age. The people that were there moved out. If you're going to stay in town we can go look at it tomorrow. I'd go now but got to be in court in the next hour. Can we meet at my house this evening?"

"If it's okay with Sandy?" I said, looking at her.

"Okay with me, I need to buy myself and Mary Ann some clothes. That's the only thing I have to do today. Shouldn't take long."

"Good. I'll have my assistant take some pictures to show you the house. We can have dinner and reminisce some. I'll have my son Bret stop by, too, if it's alright with you. He's our police chief now. You can tell him about the bad guys."

"I remember him. He was always saying he wanted to be a

policeman," I said.

"He did from the time he was seven years old. Now he's the main dude," Garrett said and laughed. "Your house doesn't have any furniture and I don't want you to stay in a motel. I got a big guest bedroom you can have and Betty can take Sandy and Mary Ann shopping in the morning."

"You still live at the same place, Garrett?"

"I do. Been there twenty-five years."

"Thank you for your help, Mr. Moore," Sandy said.

"You're very welcome," he said.

"You got a place I can put a dog?" I said. "Don't have a place to leave him."

"Sure. What kind of dog?"

"A Jack Russell terrier. I inherited him from Robert. Didn't take long for us to become buddies, but I think he likes Mary Ann more than me now."

"I'll introduce him to Betty's poodle Sapphire. I'll call her and let her know you're coming."

"Been a long time since I saw Betty. What I remember most was she was our homecoming queen the year we graduated from high school."

"Got my attention and I kept after her until we got married," Garrett said and grinned.

"We'll be there, say six, if that's okay?"

"Sounds like a plan to me," he said.

We got up, shook hands and left.

10

We got in the car, Scooter wagging his tail, licking us again.

"You have some nice friends," Sandy said.

"Yeah, we go all the way back to kindergarten," I said.

"You should stay here and I'll move on," Sandy said.

"Still got some people that want us dead. Have to solve that before either one of us can make a decision. In the meantime, you go shopping with Betty in the morning and we'll figure out what to do next. Hey there's the park. I'll let Scooter out."

"That dog don't know how lucky he is you came along," Sandy said.

"We needed each other," I said.

"How about me," Sandy said?

"Most of your troubles have come because you're with me."

I turned off on Parkway, drove down behind a tree with the

view blocked to the highway. Stopped, let Scooter and Mary Ann out so she could watch him. He smelled around for the right spot and finally peed. Mary Ann picked him up and they got back in the car. For some reason I kept looking out the window like it was something I had to do.

"Okay, Clark, we can go," Sandy said.

I couldn't move.

"Clark, let's go," she said again.

I still couldn't move.

"Clark," she said for the third time and shook my shoulder. "What's wrong?"

I was frozen in place, staring into nowhere, nothing worked on my body. I couldn't move my arms or legs. Sandy jumped out of the car, ran around to the driver side and opened the door. I could see her but it was like I was looking through her. She shook me again, yelling, "Clark! Clark!"

Suddenly I was back. I could move my arms and legs. The trance was gone as fast as it came. Sandy was holding on to me crying.

"I'm okay," I said and put my arms around her.

"The doctor said you could have some of these kinds of spells and you just did. You want me to drive?"

"Yeah would be better right now." I got out, walked around to the passenger side, staggering a little. I got in and she closed the door and looked at me.

"How you doing?" she asked.

"It's gone except for a headache," I said.

"Where we going?"

"Let's run by the house, see what it looks like. Garrett wants some work done on it."

"Okay, just tell me as we go," she said and drove back to the highway.

"Take a left. We'll come to a street named Avalon in about a mile, turn right, second house on the right. Garrett said the people that were leasing moved out. I got a key if they didn't change the lock."

"Did they know who owned the house," she said.

"No," I said.

Sandy nodded and kept driving. We came to Avalon, she turned on the street and drove in on the driveway.

"This it," she said.

"Yep," I said. "Two acres. Looks like it needs painting."

"Nice, Ranch style," she said. "Plenty of room and a fenced yard."

"Mary and I lived here after I retired for about ten years before the car wreck. First time I been back in six years. Couldn't stay and couldn't come to sell it."

"I been thinking, Clark," Sandy said. "I'm not leaving. You need me, too."

My phone rang. It was Goodnight.

"How you doing, Clark," he said.

"Having some seizures from the Trilene I told you about, but okay now."

"I called to tell you your enemies are getting fewer by eliminating themselves. Brandon has been arrested for the murder of his brother. The FBI found a camera hidden in Elton Jr.'s office bookcase that showed Brandon come in and walk up to Jr. at his desk, draw a forty-five, and shot him twice in the heart. Then he calmly put the gun away and walked out.

"Sandy's ex is a person of interest for murder of his missing sister. She disappeared and Neil showed up driving her car. He said she gave it to him and left town with a guy he didn't know. Now he's disappeared. The police have a warrant for him as a person of interest. He may know where you and Sandy are. Keep a watch for him. The tag number on her car is 645 WNK NEW YORK."

"None of this surprises me," I said. "Brandon was always the black sheep of the family. He hated his half-brother with a passion and Wiggins is a sociopath."

"I have the FBI witness program working on a new identity for Sandy and Mary Ann."

"Tell her," I said and handed her the phone on speaker.

"Talk to Goodnight."

"Hi Sonny," she said.

"Sandy, I can get you in the FBI witness program with a new identity."

"I don't want it. I'm staying with Clark until he gets medical help with his seizures.

"Look, this wasn't easy to do. I may not can do it again."

"I appreciate it but I'm not leaving him," she said.

"You don't want it?" Goodnight said.

"No, I'll take my chances with Clark."

"Put him back on the phone," he said.

"I heard," I said. "Sorry I pushed you so much to do it."

"It's okay," he said. "May be better if she does stay with you."

"Yeah" I said.

"Go see another doctor," he said.

"I will. You take care and tell Julie and the boys we said hello."

"You bet. Talk to you later, bye."

"Goodnight said they arrested Brandon for his brother's murder. Found a video of Brandon killing him and they have a warrant out for your ex as a person of interest for the disappearance of his sister."

"I think he killed her," she said.

"We may have to kill him," I said.

"Maybe they will arrest him," she said.

"Hope so," I said. "We'll stay in Brookville if you know Mary and Cooper are never going to leave me."

"I do. It's alright," she said.

"Seen the house, don't think we need to go in. I'll talk to Garrett about it tonight. I'll drive now and take you on a tour of the town. Got a mall you and Betty can go to."

I got under the wheel and drove to my old school and several other places.

I turned off the interstate highway and drove to my dad's old place. Never sold it, either. It had run down to the point it had a danger tag on it and a city demolish red certificate on the front door.

"What're you going to do about that," Sandy said.

"Nothing now, not worth saving."

"What did your dad do? You have never said anything about him or your mom."

"Just hurts too much to talk about them. They both died at the peak of life. He spent three years in the Army, served a tour in Korea. Was a hero at the battle of Huron, nominated for the medal of honor, came home and started a real-estate business. Was a millionaire by the time he was forty. Developed Parkinson's disease and died. Mom lived ten years longer then came down with cancer and passed away two years later. I was an only son like Cooper. I have always had a grievance with god for what he did."

"You shouldn't have. They had more than most. Lost mine about the same way before they should have gone. Life's not fair," she said.

"I keep telling myself that but it never changes in my mind. Same as Mary and Cooper. That's why I don't like to talk about it."

"There is a good side — you're rich," she said.

"Not exactly. I donated it to a trust fund for scholarships at my high school. Already had enough for my needs. Something happens to me, get your money from my account and disappear. Keep it between you and Sonny. I don't trust the FBI."

"Okay, I'll change the subject. You and Garrett were high school football stars there right?"

"I guess you could say that. Garrett got a scholarship, played quarterback in college. Even had some interest from the pros. High school was it for me. Got my congressman to nominate me for West Point and Cooper followed the same path until he was killed. My turn to change the subject. What would you think if I declared Mary Ann the sole owner of Scooter? She takes care of him all the time and he seems more satisfied with her than me."

"I want him forever," Mary Ann said.

"Looks like he is already. Okay, Clark, you're relieved of the responsibility," she said and smiled.

"Your mine now," Mary Ann said, looking at Scooter. He stared at her and twisted his head.

A police cruiser pulled up behind us in the driveway. Bret got out wearing his police chief uniform. He was as tall as his daddy and well built. In his early forties, as I remembered, almost ten years older than Cooper would have been. I opened the car door and got out.

"Hi Bret, was taking a look at the house. Does need some work," I said.

"Thought you may be here. Can't stay very log anyway. One of my patrolman saw a D.C. car come into town last night. Wasn't the plate number you gave me, though. Ran a check on it. Belonged to a Joseph Sanfini. No warrants or rap sheet on him. Had no legal reason to stop him. Thought I better tell you in person. I notified the FBI and we put a watch on it."

"He has a mob name I know well," I said. "One of them cut off my little finger."

"I saw the finger was missing but thought not to ask you about it. Might offend you," Bret said.

"It wouldn't have. Don't think he and Wiggins know each other but he may have come from someone Junior and Brandon knew. Parker Junior had his thumb on the Sanfini mob. They did what he said. They murdered Robert, his wife and son. Pepper's the only one left. She's a former special ops soldier and a lawyer. Can take care of herself and has a fiancé that can hold his own with anybody. My main problem now is the Trilene they gave me. Have to deal with epilepsy and some spills I never knew about. The guy you spotted may be a nephew or grandson There was a Sanfini, with the same name, that got ran over by a train when he and another one was chasing me. If he's in town he's here for one reason. To kill me and Sandy."

"Got an idea. Why don't you stay at our lake house until we get things under control?"

"Don't want to put you out," I said.

"Dad hasn't been there in a while and my wife and I got divorced two years ago. She couldn't handle me being a cop."

"Can we take Scooter?" Mary Ann said.

"Sure," Bret said. "Got a fenced backyard where you can take him when he needs to go."

Sandy looked at me. "What do you think," she said.

"Be the best thing to do," I said.

"I'll set up a watch for the lake house."

"Okay," I said.

"Follow me," he said and headed for the cruiser. I got back in the car.

"Don't say anything about the weapons we have on us." I said.

She looked at her purse. I shook my head no. She frowned and nodded okay. I could tell by her expression she didn't agree with me about the guns but she didn't say anything. I knew it was wrong not to tell Bret about the weapons. But it could be even worse if we didn't have them. I assumed Sandy still had Wiggins' Colt in her purse. I had a .357 strapped to my ankle, a small 9mm automatic in a waist holster in the curve of my back, and loose bullets for both in my pockets.

11

Bret drove to the lake, turned into a gate protected subdivision, made another turn on a street and drove in on a driveway in front of a good sized brick house with a boat house and a speed boat hanging from a lift beside it.

The first thing I thought of was the boat gave us another way to escape. And a second thought, that it also gave someone another way to us.

Bret called in his location and cut the engine. We all got out. He unlocked the front door and we went in.

"There's two bedrooms, take your pick. You can stay for as long you need to. Help yourself to anything in the fridge. The place is wired. I keep it on all the time. No one can get in without the alarm going off, including the attic. A patrol will be coming by every hour until we find out who's in town and why. Here's my card, I'll give you another one. Write yours and Sandy's phone number on it for me."

He handed me the two cards. I wrote our number on one and handed it to him, stuck the other one in my pocket with his number.

"I can see why you're the police chief," I said.

"Thanks, but I have to admit my dad's influence helped. He's the mayor," Bret said.

"I didn't know he was the mayor. He didn't say anything about it."

"Was elected for a fourth term last year."

"That son of a gun. Bet he's a good one," I said.

"He keeps getting elected so I guess he is."

"I'll talk to him about it tonight. You going to come over?"

"Going to try," Bret said. "Make yourself at home. I have some paperwork to do at the station. Should have things under control for you soon and you can go back to your house."

"I think you will," I said. "Wish I would have had your kind of help before."

"Take care," he said.

We shook hands and he left. I drew the blinds closed and we found the bedrooms.

"You and Mary take this one," I said and opened the door. "I'll take the one at the end of the hall. I'm having trouble with the Trilene, don't want you looking at me. I'll tap on the door three times if I want in."

"You going to be alright by yourself?" Sandy said.

"Yeah," I said. "Lock the door."

"I can stay with you."

Mary Ann and Scooter ran past Sandy into the bedroom.

"I'm still on a merry-go-round with the spills. I have a feeling our enemies are here watching the local cops as much as they are watching them. Just a matter of time till they find us. If it comes down to just you, all you have to do is point that gun you got in your purse and pull the trigger."

"I don't think I can do that," Sandy said.

"You may not have a choice if I go down."

"You're scaring the hell out of me."

"You have to be brave. You won't get a second chance."

Sandy opened her purse, looked at the Colt, sighed and closed the purse.

"I'll try." She went in the room and I heard the lock snap.

I started walking down the hall and a pain hit me in the head like a sledgehammer. I staggered against the wall, reached in my pocket and took out my medicine bottle and swallowed a pill, leaning against the wall for a few seconds and stumbled down the hall to the bedroom. I took my pistols out of their holsters and stuck them in the front of my belt to get to them quick.

I laid down and dozed another three hours until it was time to go to Garrett's.

My headache had slowed down. The pill was working. I had survived another kind of spill I hadn't had before. I never know what's next.

I went to the bathroom, turned on the water in the sink, cupped my hands and let water run into them, splashing it on my face. I was having trouble with my vision blurring, my hands shaking.

I took another pill.

I was in no condition to protect Sandy, her baby or myself.

My phone rang. It was Bret.

"Clark, I just got a call that two of my officers were ambushed. May be dead," he said. "There's two or three suspects. They stole the cruiser. May know where the house is. Get the girls and barricade the den. We're on our way. There's a key to the gun cabinet in my top drawer of the desk, a twelve-gauge pump shotgun in the cabinet with ammo. I have an ambulance coming, too."

"Hurry," I said.

I tapped on Sandy's door and she opened it.

"Bret thinks they're coming for us. Let's go to the den. He said he's got a shotgun in a cabinet there. After I get the gun I'm going back out. Lock the den doors. Keep Mary Ann and the dog quiet. Hold his mouth if you have to. I'll wait for them in the foyer, go."

She grabbed Mary Ann and ran to the den, Scooter following. I found the key to the gun cabinet, took the pump twelve-gauge out, found a box of buckshot and loaded the shotgun with shaking hands. This was about all I could handle now with blurred vision.

The door bell rang.

"Stay here and lock the door," I said and staggered out of the den with the shotgun. That can't be Bret, I thought, he couldn't get here that quick. I saw a man at the front door dressed in a policeman's uniform. I pressed the shotgun against my side to keep from dropping it with my shaking hands. When no one answered the doorbell he opened fire, blowing the lock apart, and pushed the door open, stepping inside. The alarm went off, screaming through the house.

Sandy opened the den door and I motioned for her to get back in. She did.

The phony policeman fired a shot at me. I pumped three rounds into him, blowing him back out the open door. Another man came running down the hall. I propped myself up against the wall and blasted him apart with three more rounds. He fell face-down on the floor, one of his arms hanging on his body by two or three veins, blood running out from beneath him.

I opened my medicine bottle for more pills but my legs gave way and I slid to the floor. I dropped the bottle as I fell and the pills spilled across the floor.

I heard footsteps on the porch and Neil Wiggins stepped over the dead guy, walked through the open door with an AR-15 and saw me on the floor. He smashed the alarm box inside the door and it shut off. I tried to raise the shotgun. He ran to me and knocked it out of my shaking hands, saw the guns in my belt. I was too weak to move. He snatched the guns from my belt and threw them across the room. He kicked me against the wall, pointed the AR-15 at me.

"Did you know the Sanfini brothers you blew away put the

Trilene in the vents in France?" He saw the surprise in my eyes. "You didn't know," he said and laughed. "Where's the bitch? I want her to see me kill you before I do her."

Sandy slid open the den doors.

"I could hear you," she said. She was standing in the open part of the doors.

"I come to kill you but it looks like I get two for one."

"No, don't hurt her," I said. "It's my fault."

"It is," he said. He pulled the slide back on the AR-15.

Scooter barked.

"I guess I got a dog to kill, too."

"Your daughter's in here, Neil."

"My daughter? May not be mine. Could be anyone's, including this piece of shit here," he said, waving the AR-15 at me.

"You know that's not true. She's your daughter."

"I'll consider that before I kill her," he said.

"You murdered your sister, didn't you," Sandy said.

"She wouldn't give me the car," he said and looked down at me.

"Thank you for killing Joe and Eddy, McKay. All the money's mine now when I get rid of you and the slut. Adios, asshole," he said as he pointed the AR-15 at me.

In the next instance, Sandy raised the Colt in a flash from her side and started pulling the trigger as fast as she could. Her first two shots hit Neil in the chest and arm. He dropped the AR-15 and fell to his knees. She kept pulling the trigger three more times. One bullet went through his eye, one hit his shoulder. She missed with the last shot. He crumbled to the floor from his knees, blood gushing out of his body. She dropped the revolver, jarring the cylinder open, the last bullet still in his gun.

I raised my arm slightly with a thumbs up. She ran to me, sat down on the floor and lifted my head up in her lap. Mary Ann and Scooter ran out of the den to us, Scooter barking his head off.

I gasped for breath. The sound of sirens could be heard in the distance.

"They're coming," she said. "Hang on."

I felt a painful quiver run though my body. I could barely make out her face with my blurred vision. I used the last energy I had to raise my hand to touch her lips with my finger so she would know I was thinking of her.

The sound of the sirens became a loud whine as they all drove up to the house. I could see shadows running thru the door. One stopped to look at the dead guy on the porch, the other one to me and a third to the guy in the hall. Don't know about Wiggins.

I heard a voice say, "There will be no more tomorrows."

Darkness covered my eyes.

I couldn't feel the beat of my heart.

A peace came over me I had never known before.

EPILOGUE

Bret came running to Sandy.

"I was waiting for you at Dad's when I got the call," he said.

She raised her head up and looked at Bret.

"He didn't get shot," she said. "He's dead from what they had already done to him. Neil said they were the ones that poisoned him with the Trilene in France. He got his revenge, though, killed them both. I shot Neil with his own gun."

"You did?" Bret said. "That the gun there in the den doorway?"

"That's it," she said.

Bret walked over to the gun, stuck a pencil in the barrel, picked it up and saw the last bullet in the open cylinder.

The medics wheeled a gurney in beside her. She got up. They put Clark on it. She bent down kissed him on the mouth.

"I love you," she said and they wheeled him out the door.

"We have to go, Sandy," Bret said.

"I'm I going to jail?"

"No, I'm going to take you to my dad's. You can stay there until we sort this out."

She motioned for Mary Ann to come to her and Scooter followed.

Three days later, the sound of Taps ended the funeral for Clark McKay.

Pepper had arranged the ceremony.

The honor guard draped an American flag over his coffin, fired a volley of rounds for a she colonel before taps.

Billie, her boyfriend Clarence, Sandy, Mary Ann, Pepper, Matt, Sonny and his family, Garrett, Bret, Betty, Dewey and his family were all sitting on the front row as family members. They had left Scooter at Garrett's place.

A large crowed from Brookville that remembered Clark attended the funeral.

They handed the folded flag from Clark's coffin to Sandy as she was the closest kin, per Billie's request knowing what they had been through together.

Everyone got up from the family row when Sandy stood up with the flag. Bret walked over to her.

"Wanted you to know there won't be any charges for killing Neil Wiggins. I filed a report saying it was self-defense. That will be the end of it."

"Thank you," she said. Garrett was standing next to Bret.

"You did the right thing," Garrett said. "What are you going to do now?"

"I think what Clark said I should. Disappear, become someone else and raise my daughter in peace and take care of Clark's friend Scooter with Sonny's help. Leave the FBI out of it. I don't trust them any more than Clark did."

"We're going to miss him," Garrett said. "There's one last

thing I need you to do before you leave. He made out a will to give the house money from both houses and his money to the high school trust fund. I would like you to stop by and witness the transactions and take the inheritance document to Dewey and collect your money. If you change your mind and decide to come back you're always welcome."

"Thank you," Sandy said. "Pepper and I have set up a code to contact each other. We may get together next year to visit Clark and his family. If we do I'll let you know."

"I would like that," Garrett said.

"Clark will too," she said and smiled. "This flag means so much to me because it meant so much to him."

"Yeah, he gave his life defending it," Garrett said. "Goodbye. I hope everything turns out well for you."

"Thanks to Clark, I think it will."

THE END

ABOUT THE AUTHOR

John L. Lansdale was born and raised in east Texas. He is married to the love of his life Mary. They have four children. He is a retired Army reserve psychological operations officer and a combat veteran that served three tours in Vietnam with numerous medals and awards. He is a graduate of a Texas police academy and a state certified peace officer. He is an inventor, country music songwriter, performer and television programmer. He produced the television special "Ladies of Country Music" and several other programs. He goes back to the Sun Record days and was introduced to Elvis Presley by Mary on their first date when Elvis was a seventeen-year-old student at Humes High School in Memphis and a ticket-taker at Loew's State Theater.

John has produced a variety of albums and music videos for country artists in Nashville along with songs for movies, with one as recently as 2018 titled "Tremble" for an upcoming film. He has hosted his own radio shows and won awards for radio and television commercials. He was a writer and editor for a business newspaper. He has worked as a comic book writer for Tales from the Crypt, IDW, Grave Tales, Cemetery Dance and many more. He co-authored Shadows West and Hell's Bounty with his brother Joe. He is the author of Slow Bullet, the four-part Mecana detective series, Long Walk Home, Zombie Gold and several others.

John's novel Slow Bullet was reviewed by Publishers Weekly as a must read page-turner with constant action and compared his work to that of popular 1950s author Mickey Spillane. The novel Long Walk Home was a finalist in the fiction category for the National Indie Excellence Awards. The novel Zombie Gold received great reviews including a Booklist review that praised it as a superb story with characters that came alive. Kissing the Devil received praise as a pulp novella. All titles are still in print with new ones on the way.

John was recently inducted into the Gladewater Museum. His motto is: Never Give Up.

SLOW BULLET - AN EXCERPT

The sound of Huey Helicopters in the distance meant the beginning. The ironic part was I never felt more alive than when I faced death. I checked my ammo and loaded a full magazine into my M-16. The barrel was cold and damp from a long night of silence. A slow wind brought a lingering smell of garlic that told me Charlie had arrived.

The rising sun silhouetted the hoard of gunships in the morning sky as they fired rockets at enemy positions. The screams of death fueled my basic instincts of survival and a feeling of exhilaration flooded my mind. Better him than me. I heard the dreaded sound of an incoming mortar round that exploded a few feet from me. The concussion of the blast knocked me down. I checked all my body parts. I didn't see any blood, but my ears wouldn't stop ringing. I put my hands over my ears and the ringing still wouldn't stop.

My eyes popped open. I was in bed, the phone ringing. My pulse was racing, my brain speeding through a forty-year corridor from past to present. I switched on a lamp and fumbled on the table for my cell phone. I knocked an open bottle of Jack Daniels off the table and spilled most of it on the floor. I took a deep breath and said, "Hello."

THE MECANA SERIES

All titles available individually or compiled in *The Complete Files of Detective Thomas Mecana* compendium.

Book #1 -- HORSE OF A DIFFERENT COLOR
Dallas PD Detective Thomas Mecana is on the hunt for a serial killer terrorizing the Lone Star State. Joining him is Darcie Connors, a young officer working her first murder case. With hard work, and some luck, Mecana and his partner discover a most-unusual serial killer case with murder in its very genes.

Book #2 -- WHEN THE NIGHT BIRD SINGS
Detectives Thomas Mecana and Darcie Connors are on the trail of a new suspect. With an ever-growing suspect list, Mecana must toe the line between friend and foe. Each action leaves them sitting in the crosshairs of danger. One wrong move could mean the end.

Book #3 -- TWISTED JUSTICE
Dallas Homicide Detective Sunday Verves is looking into the suspicious deaths of local drug runners when she discovers a potential suspect that hits too close to home. When the trail leads her south of the border, she enlists some old friends to track down the suspects.

Book #4 -- THE BOX
Detective Thomas Mecana and the gang get back together for another case. Mecana soon finds the case is bringing back old evidence. This horror-filled novel brings the Mecana Series full-circle to where it all began.

OTHER TITLES BY JOHN

BROKEN MOON

Billie Jo Dobbs was born to a Cheyenne mother and a US Marshal father. After an attack claiming her mother's life, she moves to Kansas with her father to start over. Years later in 1876, her father is ambushed at their homestead. With his dying breath he warns Billie Jo, saving her life. She flees to a nearby town looking for a few friendly faces to ride with her to the Cheyenne territory in Montana to find her former tribe.

LONG WALK HOME

The O'Rourke family lives on a fading farm in the small town of Angel Point, Mississippi. With family, friends and neighbors fighting overseas in WWII - and rising racial tensions back home - the summer of 1944 turns into a nightmare of murder and loss. Trenton O'Rourke reflects on those days and how his life was forever changed.

THE LAST GOOD DAY

As the Civil War draws to a close, Major Rance Allison is wounded in one of its last battles. He later awakens in an enemy field hospital only to find out he is now on the same side as those he was fighting. The war is over. Missing a limb, his home and his family, Rance sets out to find a new life for himself.

BOY AND HOG / BOY AND HOG RETURN

In the deep woods, anything can happen. A group of white-collar workers with a hand-drawn map trek into the wilderness for a hunting expedition. But out there, will they be the hunters or the prey? Also found in the collection *Beyond Imagination*.

EMERGENCY CHRISTMAS

Join the Albright family and the guest who surprises them just in time for the holiday. Along the way, they discover sometimes crisis brings a family closer together.

JOHN L. LANSDALE TITLES AVAILABLE FROM BOOKVOICE PUBLISHING

-Broken Moon (Hardcover - eBook)
-The Last Good Day (Hardcover - eBook)
-Long Walk Home (Hardcover - Paperback - eBook)
-Beyond Imagination (Hardcover - Paperback - eBook)
-Kissing the Devil (Hardcover - Paperback - eBook)
-Slow Bullet (Hardcover - Paperback - eBook)
-The Complete Files of Detective Thomas Mecana (Paperback - eBook)
-Horse of a Different Color (Hardcover - Paperback - eBook)
-When the Night Bird Sings (Paperback - eBook)
-Twisted Justice (Paperback - eBook)
-The Box (Paperback - eBook)
-Zombie Gold (Paperback - eBook)
-Emergency Christmas (Audiobook - Chapbook - eBook)
-Hell's Bounty [with Joe R. Lansdale] (Paperback - eBook)

STAY CONNECTED
WITH
BOOKVOICE PUBLISHING
AND
JOHN L. LANSDALE

www.bookvoicepublishing.com